Farthingales is Aunt Amethyst.

The children agreed on that.

She was trying valiantly to save the gabled old house in the English countryside, which was beset by taxes and falling into ruin. From the first day of their visit, Caroline, Richard, and Kit were determined to help—and they soon found that the beautiful snowstorm paperweight on the library mantel held the key. When the sun shone on it in a special way, time and space were suddenly suspended and the children found themselves confronted by ancestors from bygone eras, including Michael, the boy who came from the year 1832 to meet them in the present—ancestors who held the secret of the ruin of Farthingales.

THE SNOWSTORM is a charming and exciting story, peopled by vibrant characters whose personalities, regardless of their era, are very real and very much alive. And as the mystery unfolds, one learns the importance of tradition in maintaining identity and how many traditions are still a part of family life.

COVER AND TITLE PAGE ILLUSTRATIONS BY JOSEPH SCHINDELMAN

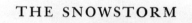

THE SNOWSTORM

THE SNOWSTORM

by Beryl Netherclift

ALFRED A. KNOPF : NEW YORK

Acknowledgments

The author acknowledges with thanks permission from Sidgwick and Jackson, Ltd. for the quotation from John Drinkwater's poem "Moonlight Apples," which appears on page 44 and also Ernest Benn, Ltd. for the quotation from *The Story of the Amulet* by E. Nesbit, which appears on page 145.

THIS IS A BORZOI BOOK
PUBLISHED BY ALFRED A. KNOPF, INC.

For Irene,
who gave me the snowstorm

CONTENTS

THE SNOWSTORM

Chapter *1*

AUNT AMETHYST

"So," said Mother to her old schoolfriend, Mrs. Tressider, "we shall be gone three months. We're not going by air. The doctor says Neil needs a sea voyage, so we decided to go by boat. Then we fly over to Bermuda from New York."

The wind shuddered and shrieked outside; the curtains billowed out and a flutter of rain came down the chimney. "We shall be gone three months," repeated Mother, patiently wiping the spattered hearth tiles, "missing all this sort of thing and basking, we hope, in warm sunshine. There's nothing so delightful to leave behind," pronounced Mother with satisfaction, "as an English January."

"Quite so. I do agree, dear. But what," asked Mrs.

Tressider, thoughtfully helping herself to a third piece of hot buttered toast, "what are you going to do with the children?"

The children, Caroline, Kit, and Richard, pricked up their ears. Chunky, the springer spaniel, pricked his up too, because naturally wherever the twins and Richard went, he went also.

"The children?" echoed Mother vaguely, as if she had forgotten she had any such encumbrances, let alone that the three of them were here beside the hearth with her. "Oh, the *children*. . . . Push the serving cart a bit nearer, Kit dear, will you? . . . The children . . . " (And they all held their breath.) "The children are going to Aunt Amethyst Faraday at Farthingales. . . ."

Well, that was the first they had heard of it. That was the first they had heard of their Aunt Amethyst, too. And Farthingales.

"Aunt Amethyst? Oh, yes, I remember her," recollected Mrs. Tressider, taking a flapjack from the cart. "*Your* aunt, of course. The children's great-aunt . . . She came to your wedding—a beautiful woman."

"Like a piece of Dresden china," nodded Mother happily. "Yes. . . . Well, Farthingales belongs to Aunt Amethyst now, since my grandfather died. It will be just the place for the children. Devonshire, you know. On the edge of the moors. Miles away from anywhere. It will do them a world of good," said Mother fondly, looking around the ring of expectant faces, "to get away from civilization for a bit. At Farthingales they can run wild."

Farthingales! Was there ever a place like it?

"*When I die,*" *Caroline was to say later, very solemnly,* "*you'll find Farthingales written on my heart, just like . . . just like . . .*"

"*Mary Queen of Scots,*" *supplied Kit, knowledgeably.*

"*Yes.*"

Richard whistled. "*By golly—when you die . . . And you only twelve-and-a-half! Why, it'll be scribbled all over at the rate you're going. The other day you said it would be Chunky written there.*"

"*Well, and what if I did? There's room for both,*" *asserted Caroline with dignity.* "*I'm a large-hearted person.*"

"*What about Aunt Amethyst?*" *reminded Kit slyly.*

"*Farthingales is Aunt Amethyst,*" *replied her twin loftily.*

The last word had been said. Farthingales was indeed Aunt Amethyst. Moreover, Aunt Amethyst was Farthingales.

"Why didn't you tell us?" they asked their mother that evening after Mrs. Tressider had gone.

"I didn't tell you because . . . Well, just because," replied Mother mysteriously. "For one thing, after his illness, your father wasn't sure until today that this business trip was really coming off. And then, for another, I couldn't be certain that Aunt Amethyst would be able to have you; I've been out of touch with her for so many years. . . . But I was going to tell you this evening. It was just that Mrs. Tressider got in first, as it were."

"Well, when are we going?" Kit wanted to know.
"Soon? This month? Before school starts?"

"You are going in exactly a week," smiled Mother.

A week! As near as that!

But it wasn't really so very near. . . . For first of all
there was goodness knows what to do. Covering everything up with dust sheets, for example, and notifying the
tradespeople, and shutting up the house. Not to mention
packing, and seeing off their parents, and spending the
last night with Mrs. Tressider.

At last, however, the auspicious day had come, and it
was bright and sunny, and much warmer. "It will be a
really delightful journey," purred Mrs. Tressider, "and I
have packed you a good lunch, so you ought to be all
right. Now don't forget, will you? You are being met
at Up Moor Station with a car, and here is a postcard
telling me you've arrived safely. I want you to post it
as soon as you get there."

The train left Paddington Station at nine o'clock and
to their chagrin Mrs. Tressider put them in the care of
the guard.

"It's unfair," growled Richard. "By golly, I won't
let her forget this. Me eleven and you over twelve."

The guard turned out to be quite a good sort, however,
and when they had to change at the junction onto a
branch line he not only superintended the move and
settled them into a carriage which would, he said, be
out of reach of the smoke and smut from the engine so
that they could hang out of the window in comfort, but
was also full of agreeable bits of advice, such as which

side to look out if they wanted to see the sea, where to throw out their orange peel if they *must* (only they hadn't any oranges), and not to trust their weight to the luggage racks if they wanted to arrive at Up Moor intact.

"Now, mind ye," finished up the kindly old man, "Up Moor is the fifth stop. And by that time it'll be getting dusk so ye'd best all hop out pretty sharp or one of ye may get left behind."

"Well, that's not likely to be me," vowed Richard as the train moved off.

And indeed it wasn't for, when the ancient locomotive lurched to a standstill for the fifth time, Richard already had the door open and was deposited upon the platform head first.

"Gosh!" exclaimed Kit. "Have you hurt yourself, Rick?"

"Of course not!" scoffed Richard, with the blood streaming down his face. "Hurry up now. Hand me that luggage."

Helter-skelter, they bundled everything out, jumping down after it just as the train, with a raucous whistle of farewell, bustled off importantly into the darkness.

"The old boy was right. No time wasted here," observed Richard, pulling out his handkerchief and attempting to clean up his face. "No, leave me alone for heaven's sake," as Caroline and Kit offered to help. "We can't bother about trifles. If we're being met with a car we've got to find it."

There seemed to be no one about, but a dim glimmer of gaslight showed from a huddle of small buildings down the platform and they made their way hopefully toward it. At the same time, however, a rattling old station wagon came grinding and screeching into the station yard, and a tall gaunt figure in rubber boots and trousers and a shabby suède windbreaker jumped out.

"Are you the Winthrop children?" a voice hailed them. (As if it weren't perfectly obvious, as Kit said afterwards, for there were no other children to be seen.)

"Yes," spoke up Richard as the man of the family, "we are," and he went forward politely with extended hand. "Are you from our Aunt Amethyst?"

"I *am* your Aunt Amethyst," said the voice briskly. "Now tumble in, all of you, and don't sit on that brace of rabbits on the back seat. I hope you're going to be happy and quite comfortable at Farthingales, I'm sure, but mind you, I can't help it if you're not. Is that your dog? I hope he's going to get on all right with Fauntleroy. Your mother didn't mention a dog in her letter."

"Oh, Chunky always goes where we go," explained Richard apologetically. "But he's very well behaved."

"Humph!" said Aunt Amethyst, and then she turned to look more closely at her great-nephew. "Humph . . ." she said again, and her voice trailed off uncertainly.

"I never cared much for boys," Aunt Amethyst told Caroline and Kit years later. "Never seemed to get on with 'em at all, except my own two brothers. But young Richard endeared himself to me from the start, with that bleeding nose and the great gash in his forehead he was trying to hide under his cap! Of course, I pretended not to notice either—I know boys."

Richard was offered, and accepted, a seat next to Aunt

Amethyst. Caroline and Kit packed themselves in behind with Chunky, not to mention the dead rabbits, and they were off.

For seemingly endless miles they drove up hill and tore down dale, took continuous hairpin bends on two wheels, and rumbled like thunder over bridges. Every so often there was the glint of a river beside the road, and once they plunged noisily through a puddle. Then, at last, there was a straight line of scrunchy, bumpy gravel drive beneath over-arching trees, and finally the outline of a house with steep gables and tall chimney stacks standing up mysteriously against the sky.

"Ah, Fauntleroy evidently heard us coming," smiled Aunt Amethyst as the car rattled to a stop in front of a flight of shallow steps leading up to an open lamplit doorway. "Out you get, children—and welcome to Farthingales! Later on I'm going to paste up in your rooms a list of all the things you should know about the place, but for now—we'll have some supper, eh?"

"Well, we're really hungry," admitted Richard frankly. "Nothing really substantial since breakfast, and then only herrings." (Richard disliked herrings.) "Is Fauntleroy your butler or something?"

"This is Fauntleroy," said Aunt Amethyst, putting her hand affectionately on the head of a massive golden labrador standing hospitably on the threshold. "Better than any butler, I assure you."

Fauntleroy waved his tail with slow dignity and came forward modestly onto the porch. Chunky, suddenly catching sight of him, bounded forward with his usual enthusiastic friendliness, and there was a moment of deep suspense while Fauntleroy stiffened with aristocratic hauteur and the children held their breath. But "Thank goodness," as Kit muttered to Caroline, after a little preliminary sniffing and circling, the two seemed to establish a tacit understanding and trotted off happily together in the direction, presumably, of the kitchen.

"Of course, he has his limitations," confessed Aunt Amethyst, looking apologetically after Fauntleroy. "For example, you'll have to carry up your own bags, I'm afraid. . . . Still, you girls can't miss your room—the door is standing open, just down the passage, and Richard's is the one beyond. When you're ready, come down and lend me a hand with the fire, will you? I'm not awfully bright at lighting fires." And their great-aunt vanished.

The children looked around them curiously. They were in a long, lofty hall, stone-walled and stone-floored, with a great arched window reaching from floor to ceiling on either side of the door and a stone-manteled Tudor fireplace on the left. Ahead of them on the right was an oak staircase.

Richard took a case in each hand and staggered toward it, Caroline and Kit following close behind with the remaining two.

"I hope you don't mind mice," was Aunt Amethyst's parting shot from some invisible hinterland as they climbed the wide, shining stairs. "You'll see quite a few around, most likely, because we haven't got a cat at the moment. But don't worry. They won't bite you, and the little mites are welcome as long as they know their place."

"Golly!" whispered Kit, when they were safely out of earshot, "What a place! It's simply fantastic! What next, I wonder!"

"Do you think Mother realized?" returned Caroline.

Kit shook her head. "I guess she hadn't a clue. Fortunately," she added, "for I wouldn't have missed this for *anything*—it's simply fantastic! Hello . . . What on earth's happened to Rick?"

Well might she have asked, for poor Richard, having reached the threshold of the girls' bedroom, had suddenly slumped across the two suitcases in a dead faint.

What happened next nobody could quite remember afterwards. "We must have called out, I suppose," said Kit.

But suddenly there was Aunt Amethyst down on her knees beside the fallen warrior, deftly loosening his tie and unbuttoning his collar.

"Water—quickly!" She pointed to an old-fashioned washstand in the girls' room.

Kit ran to the large china pitcher and lifted it down, Caroline brought the basin, and they all splashed water over Richard with energy and enthusiasm.

"The wonder *is*," observed Aunt Amethyst darkly as she splashed, "that it didn't happen before. I had my eye on him in the car all the time. I had my eye on him more than I had it on the road, to tell the truth. But he didn't bat an eyelid. He's a brave lad."

Well, it was not surprising, perhaps, that the brave lad, under all this expert attention, came around fairly quickly.

"Wow! That was a nasty one," he muttered, opening

his eyes, and sitting up determinedly. He had probably had enough female fussing, poor boy—but alas, he was doomed to frustration.

"Hurray! He's made it! We've revived him! Now for the next step—for bandages and iodine!" cried Aunt Amethyst like an incantation. "Caroline—you're nearest. That door behind you. Open it. On my dressing table you will observe a first-aid box."

For the next ten minutes the sisters looked on respectfully while Aunt Amethyst washed the dried blood from their brother's face and cleaned and dressed the gash on his forehead.

"There! Is that comfortable? Do you feel better?" She fixed the bandage with a neat reef knot and sat back on her heels to review her handiwork.

"I feel fine," Richard assured her, not without a certain amount of admiration. "I could eat a big supper now."

"Then eat it you shall," promised Aunt Amethyst. "Well, that's your room over there. Sit down now and rest in that rocking chair with the patchwork cushion and when we're ready we'll call you." She rose briskly to her feet. "Now you girls, come and lend me a hand with the fire. I'm not," confessed Aunt Amethyst again, diffidently, "awfully bright at lighting fires."

"How come you have to light them yourself?" inquired Caroline politely as they went downstairs.

"Ah," sighed Aunt Amethyst, like the first whisper of wind that foreruns a gale, "I could tell you! I could tell you all night! It's a tale of woe, indeed—a tale of death duties smacking us in the face at all the worst times, of

taxes and expenses shooting up and investments likewise
shooting down. Of repair bills piling up and the farms
failing and the dear Lord knows what else besides. . . .
But enough! We've no time to waste repining. *Tempus
fugit.* Some day, perhaps, I'll tell you more."

Aunt Amethyst opened a door off the cold stone hall
and led them into a little square, cozy room with oak-
paneled walls. The furniture was all of oak, too, and
there was a long window with a deep window seat and a
small stone fireplace where lingered the remains of a
wood fire.

"This is the anteroom," announced Aunt Amethyst,
drawing the curtains. "This is where we eat." Then she
rattled the fire irons noisily in the hearth. "Fauntleroy!"
she called loudly, "Firewood!"

Immediately there was heard a scampering sound afar
off and presently Fauntleroy burst triumphantly into the
room holding in his mouth a small basket full of sticks
with a folded newspaper and a box of matches on top.

"Good man," commended Aunt Amethyst, patting him
fondly. "Now the coal."

Fauntleroy, all but falling over Chunky, who, puzzled
but respectful, had followed him in to see what it was all
about, dashed off again, and Aunt Amethyst turned
confidentially to Caroline and Kit. "Trust a dog to know
what you want and do it without argument! Now Mrs.
Burbage . . . Oh, well, I save a lot on Mrs. Burbage, so I
won't say any more. . . . And, after all, I *have* got Mrs.
Tidy."

"Who is Mrs. Tidy?"

"Well, truth to tell, I really don't quite know," con-

fessed Aunt Amethyst, brushing out the remains of the
last fire and crumpling up newspaper for the new one.
"I suppose, actually, she's a sort of crossbreed: a daily,
a cook, and an odd-jobber all in one. She bicycles in early
every morning from a small hamlet between here and the
village; sometimes she stays and sometimes she doesn't.
I'll admit she lit this fire for me this morning, but somehow or other I forgot it and it went out. . . . Now, what's
your method? Paper—sticks—paper again? Then the
coal? Can't go far wrong there, can we?" She sighed
heavily. "But that's just where I fall down. Something
eludes me. It's not in my fingers, perhaps. Ah, here's the
coal!"—as Fauntleroy padded in, rather more slowly this
time, with a weighty basket of coal. "Look, child—*you*
try! It always dies on me. I'm not," lamented Aunt
Amethyst in now familiar strain, "awfully bright at
lighting fires."

Caroline and Kit managed the fire without any trouble
at all ("We have to light a fire with two matches at
Guides," Caroline explained), and Aunt Amethyst, de-
lighted, produced a gay cloth from a drawer and spread
it on the gate-legged table. "Now come along to the
pantry," she invited cozily, "and we'll see what we can
rake up to eat."

Caroline and Kit followed her across the hall, ex-
changing dubious and hungry glances.

"We had herrings for breakfast," uneasily ventured
Richard, who had suddenly joined the entourage, having
apparently grown tired of sitting waiting in the rocking
chair with the patchwork cushion.

Aunt Amethyst looked up in surprise but accepted

his presence without comment. "You've told me that
once already. Well, mark my words, you won't have
herrings at Farthingales, my boy, and that's certain.
Herrings cost money. My hens lay eggs free of charge,
and sure as eggs is eggs, eggs you'll have for breakfast.
Every morning, in one form or another."

Their aunt tempered her ultimatum, it is true, with
the sweetest of sweet smiles, but all three children felt it
to be an extremely fortunate thing that they were each of
them particularly partial to eggs for breakfast, or indeed
at any time of the day. For Aunt Amethyst was producing
them from the larder right now, from a great red crock
full of beautifully large brown ones.

"Nothing like eggs for children," she beamed, happily.
"We'll have omelets. Anyone know how to make an
omelet?"

That night, in their chintz-hung, candlelit bedroom,
Caroline and Kit surveyed the long day from the cozy
depths of a great four-poster luxuriantly furnished with a
feather mattress (warmed by hot-water bottles), lavender-
scented sheets, and delicious pillows.

"I don't suppose Mother would approve of the feathers
but—well, Aunt Amethyst does know what a bed ought
to be like, I will say that for her," acknowledged Kit,
scooping up a dividing ridge and blissfully snuggling
down on her side of it into seemingly bottomless depths
of warm softness.

"It's the best part of the whole day," agreed Caroline.

"Not the *best*. That was supper," protested Kit.
"Though I do say it myself, supper was wizard."

Considering the reckless number of eggs Kit had swept into the omelets that was only to be expected, of course. But certainly supper had been a meal to remember.

Aunt Amethyst had suddenly recollected, with obvious relief, a ham—a whole, splendiferous crumb-browned ham—that Mrs. Tidy had cooked for just this very occasion. Likewise curly sausage rolls and a fat apple tart liberally sprinkled with sugar had been discovered, not to mention a plate of cheese tarts and a lemon meringue pie. Mrs. Tidy had no doubt intended all these delectable items to cover more than one day, but Aunt Amethyst was suddenly in a mood to be generous and to bypass firmly any such parsimonious designs, and I fear that of the fantastic array of foodstuffs that came out of the pantry on to the table very little, if any, went back in again.

"I think I'm going to like it here," Richard had said thoughtfully at the end of the meal.

By this time it had been getting late and nobody had disagreed with Aunt Amethyst when she had pronounced it to be bedtime, for one and all were, in fact, practically asleep already.

They had washed and undressed by candlelight, for no gas or electricity had yet reached the bedrooms at Farthingales, although the lower rooms had both.

The washstand in the girls' room was a little old-fashioned white one, with a hole in the middle for the basin. "Why, of course—half the water's gone: we used it on Rick," remarked Caroline, lifting the pitcher. "What do *you* say, Aunt Amethyst? Shall we skip washing tonight?"

"Indeed you won't—not in my house," replied Aunt Amethyst dangerously. "I'll bring you all some hot water in a moment when I've looked for the towels. I make my own soap—which would you like? Lavender or violet?"

"I'd like lavender," said Caroline, "and do you think . . . could we . . . might we have a nightlight, please?"

Aunt Amethyst quite naturally looked astounded. "A *nightlight?* Great girls like you? What on earth for?"

Caroline hung her head and looked ashamed. "It's me . . . Kit doesn't mind. I'm not *afraid* of the dark, but it seems to suffocate me and I can't sleep."

"Well, nightlights cost money," observed Aunt Amethyst severely; but she looked as if she were casting about in her mind for a solution to the problem.

"We're twins, Kit and I, but we don't stress it, and we're not a *bit* alike, not in *any* way," confessed Caroline humbly. "I'm the elder—I'm the elder by six hours—but Kit is the more sensible. Kit could sleep *any*where."

"You poor child! Take that anxious frown off your face, for heaven's sake. I have the very thing. Put on your dressing gown and come downstairs with me to the lamp room."

In that small, stone-walled cell of a room off the kitchen she had lifted down from a shelf thronged with lanterns and candlesticks and old-fashioned paraffin lamps, a strange and intriguing object: a tall circular receptacle made of ancient-looking iron and pierced with small holes.

"Now, how will this do? It's what we used to call my Hundred Eyes," Aunt Amethyst had explained fondly. "We'll put a lighted candle inside and the dear thing will keep you company all night. Lie in bed, Caroline, and look at it until you fall asleep."

And that was just what Caroline was doing now as she snuggled down beside Kit—staring fascinated at the little pattern of eyes fiercely glowing in the dark. Aunt Amethyst's voice came back to her softly, kindly, mixed up with the sound of a river somewhere outside . . .

Hush . . . hush . . . "It's what children at Farthingales have been doing since Tudor days." Hush . . . hush. . . . "Yes, it's as old as that." Hush . . . hush . . . hush . . . "And I did it myself, too, for I was just the same at your age, Caroline." Hush . . . hush. . . . "But you'll grow out of it, child. You'll grow out of it." Hush . . . hush . . . hush. . . .

Chapter 2

FARTHINGALES

The next morning they were awakened early by the sound of Chunky barking outside the door, where he had spent the night on a red rug tastefully decorated with the words *"Bon Repos"* in yellow.

"Not on *any* account can I have dogs in the bedrooms," Aunt Amethyst had warned them. "Fauntleroy sleeps on a rug outside my door, so Chunky can do the same outside yours. They'll be company for each other."

Chunky had apparently slept well on his red mat and when Kit eventually opened the bedroom door he came bounding in in fine form.

"Bless him," cried Caroline, hugging him rapturously, "Did 'ums have a good night, then?"

"Chunky doesn't like that baby language—I've told

you before," admonished Richard, suddenly appearing on the threshold, and surveying the scene with lofty disapproval. "It's demoralizing. . . ." He wandered over to the window. "I was wondering if we could see the sea, but it's raining and everything's blotted out. Isn't it a bore?"

"It is," admitted Caroline, "with so much we want to do on our first day. Never mind, perhaps we'll find it clears up later. Aunt Amethyst said we were to make our own beds. Have you made yours, Rick?"

"Yes, I have. It's a jolly comfortable bed. I slept like a log."

"So did we," chorused Caroline and Kit, stripping back the sheets and shaking up the mattress. "Have you seen any mice?" added Kit.

"Not a single one." Richard looked thoughtful. "Maybe she was trying to scare us."

The girls re-spread the sheet and put back the pillows. "I *heard* them, though," said Caroline. "Scampering about overhead. There were all sorts of queer noises, actually, but they didn't keep me awake."

"There was an owl or something hooting," recollected Richard, "and that's all I remember. . . . Look, there's a piece of blanket you haven't tucked in.'

"What do you think of our bed?" Caroline asked, making all secure. "Aunt Amethyst says it's Tudor. See —it has the Tudor rose carved on the posts. I wonder if Queen Elizabeth the First ever slept in it?"

"Well, it looks grim enough for anything," chuckled Richard, "but I like the quilt."

It was a patchwork quilt with gay hexagons of silks

and velvets in all the colors of the rainbow, and it made the bed look like a great basket of exotic flowers in the otherwise simple room.

"Yes, it's pretty, isn't it? It's a pretty room altogether," agreed Kit contentedly. "Yours is nice, too, Rick, with that rocking chair and the oak furniture . . . Now where *has* my comb gone? Oh, Rick, you great oaf! You're stepping on it. Get off!"

Richard picked up the comb and turned huffily to the door. "Come along, Chunky, old man. Let's leave the women to their fussing and go down to see what there is for breakfast."

"What about your own washing?" Kit flung after him. "There's a smudge on the back of your neck and it doesn't look as if you've washed behind your ears, either."

"Rats to you," returned Richard mildly. "Come on, old boy."

Chunky obediently trotted after his master and, not to be outdone, Caroline and Kit hastily smoothed their hair and followed close behind.

"There probably won't be anyone around when you come down in the morning," Aunt Amethyst had said the night before. "I have to take some produce to market and Mrs. Tidy will have come and gone again. But get up just when you like, help yourselves to what you fancy, and amuse yourselves till I return."

The children had risen at much their usual hour and all the clocks in the house were striking eight as they went downstairs.

In the anteroom three places were laid for breakfast and a coal fire was leaping merrily up the chimney. Its cheerful glow was both welcome and inviting, for the morning was cold and dark and the rain was still pelting down as if its very life depended on it. Richard spread his hands appreciatively to the warm blaze. "What are we going to have for breakfast?"

"Well, we'd better go and see what there is first," said Caroline sensibly.

Making their way to the kitchen they found the stove roaring away briskly and a kettle on top singing happily to itself. The great raftered room made a colorful and homely picture and the children looked around it admiringly: at the polished guns over the chimneypiece, the long dresser thronged with pewter and blue china, the gay rag rugs on the red-tiled floor, the bright brass fender, and the copper pots and pans.

"Well, now to work," said Kit, rolling up her sleeves and tying on an apron she had worn the previous evening.

Aunt Amethyst had said they were to have eggs for breakfast every morning, you may recollect. But then, later on, in a rather contradictory fashion, she had said, "Help yourselves to what you fancy"—so Richard said he reckoned it would be all right if they ate up the rest of the sausage rolls and the remains of the ham as well as frying themselves some eggs.

Alas, when they reached the pantry it was discovered that Aunt Amethyst had apparently fancied the ham herself, but there was a sausage roll apiece and a few cheese tarts that would come in handy and, of course, eggs!

"Two each would be about what Aunt Amethyst had

in mind, I should think," said Richard, reflectively eyeing the red crock.

"Well . . ." demurred Caroline anxiously.

"Yes," agreed Kit briskly, "two each. That's sensible enough. Otherwise they'll all be stale before they get eaten up. Well, let's get cracking. We're having them fried, aren't we?"

Aunt Amethyst had thoughtfully put out a bowl of bacon fat for just that purpose, so presently the kitchen was full of delightful sizzly aromas and, while Kit fried the eggs at one end of the huge coal stove, Caroline got the kettle boiling at the other and made the tea.

Very soon, therefore, they were carrying a heavily laden tray back to the little anteroom—with Chunky following rather wistfully behind: he had hoped to find Fauntleroy in the kitchen but Fauntleroy had apparently gone to market with his mistress. There was no sign of him.

"What shall we do this morning?" demanded Caroline, as the meal began to show signs of coming to an end.

"I vote we go exploring," said Richard decisively.

"What—in the pouring rain!" exclaimed Kit.

"Indoors, loopy, not out. Explore the house, I mean. Any reason why we shouldn't?"

"Well, I suppose not. . . . Aunt Amethyst said 'amuse yourselves.' "

"And I'm *longing* to see what's on the other side of that door over there," agreed Caroline, looking across the room.

"Right! Let's find out!" suggested Richard, jumping up.

The door in the dark paneling opened easily and the

children gasped as a flood of light came sweeping in from a long, white-walled room with great tall windows and a gilded ceiling.

"It must be . . . yes, it *is*—the drawing room," announced Richard, standing back with the air of a showman.

"The drawing room!" echoed Caroline, hastily swallowing the last morsel of cheese tart and joining him in the doorway.

Kit chased a final piece of fried bread around her plate and followed after. "Golly. Isn't it *fantastic!* Look at the chandeliers, Caro!"

Caroline stood and looked in awed silence. The white-paneled walls, the sea-green curtains at the long windows, the sofas and chairs of a bygone age, the crystal chandeliers and the gilded mirrors, all added up to something that was, to her, almost overwhelming.

"Magic . . ." she whispered. "It doesn't look real. . . ."

But it *was* real.

They went around the room, looking at the gilt-framed pictures on the walls, peering into the elegant cabinets, trying the chairs—and the fact that everything seemed to be thick with dust and that the curtains and upholstery were faded and moth-eaten mattered not at all.

Richard paused before a harp standing in the window and ran his fingers across the strings, but no sound came from it, beyond a dry whisper.

"Look! A grand piano!" exclaimed Kit, from another window. "Oh, I wonder if Aunt Amethyst would let me play it?"

It looked as if Aunt Amethyst played it herself, for it

was the only dusted piece of furniture in the room and a pile of music lay on top of it—Chopin and Schumann and Grieg.

"You must ask her," nodded Caroline, as Kit tentatively lifted the lid and ran her fingers over the yellowed keys.

The stone fireplace was carved with cherubs and wreaths of flowers; it was a great cavernous affair, and at the moment the rain was spattering down onto the hearth just as it had done that day at home—the day they had first heard of Farthingales.

"It must look lovely when the fire is lit!" exclaimed Caroline. "Supposing we light one now and give Aunt Amethyst a surprise when she comes back from market!"

"And dust the room," added Kit, warming to the idea. "The windows need cleaning too, but maybe we wouldn't have time for those—they're so enormous."

"Well, let's start with the fire," suggested Richard. "I wonder if we can find the coal and firewood. . . ."

"We probably don't need to if Fauntleroy is anywhere about," said Kit reminiscently. She rattled the fire irons energetically. "Fauntleroy! Firewood!" she called loudly.

There was no answer—no scamper of feet far off. Fauntleroy was evidently still absent.

Then, just at that moment, Chunky, who had been looking out of one of the windows, broke into a loud and excited barking.

"It's no use calling for Fauntleroy in here," said Caroline, going to see what it was all about. "He's away out there."

And sure enough there *was* Fauntleroy, trotting briskly

up the avenue in the rain. He wore a smart, red water-proof cover over his back, strapped neatly in two places underneath him, and in his mouth he carried a basket with a waterproof cover that matched his own. He was making for the side of the house—presumably the kitchen door.

"Let's go and meet him and see what he has in the basket," suggested Richard, immediately forgetting about the fire.

Probably Richard was anticipating edible goods, but Fauntleroy's cargo, when they opened the back door and found him shaking off the rain on the porch, was discovered to be a tin of shoe polish, a package of candles, a bottle of ink, *The Times,* a pair of mended shoes, and the morning's mail, mostly postcards.

"Why, look—the top one's for us!" cried Caroline.

And so it was. It was from their mother, posted just before sailing. "Hope you arrived safely. Have fun, darlings," she had written breezily.

The children glanced tentatively through the other postcards, thinking there might be a similar one for Aunt Amethyst, but there wasn't. One was to say the piano tuner would be coming at 11 A.M. tomorrow, another was advertising a sale of farm implements, and a third politely asked Miss Faraday for rummage for the local Boy Scouts.

"Huh. They ought to get a lot of that sort of stuff here," Richard observed judiciously—and there was a gleam of enthusiasm in his eye, for as a Boy Scout himself he was quick to recognize good honest rummage when he saw it.

In the meantime Fauntleroy had scraped his feet dry on the doormat and had jumped onto a stool, where he sat upright, trying to gain the children's attention and uttering little exclamations of impatience.

"He wants *something*," said Kit, puzzled, "but what can it be?"

Fauntleroy flashed his eyes scornfully and tried to reach underneath himself, but only succeeded in falling off the stool.

"Why, he wants us to undo his straps for him, of course," exclaimed Caroline, as Fauntleroy determinedly jumped up onto his perch again.

And sure enough that was the answer. As soon as he was divested of his wet garment, Fauntleroy jumped down and, picking up the discarded cover, hung it neatly over a low rail on the porch which looked as if it might have been put there for that very purpose, as indeed it had, they discovered later. "Dogs can be trained to do quite a lot for themselves—and for other people as well," Aunt Amethyst had assured them blandly the previous evening, and she had gone on to explain how it was that Fauntleroy could open the front door. There was a heavy oaken latch to it, which the ingenious animal could push up with his head; the door then swung open on its own weight, unless, of course, it had also been locked, which was not often the case during the daytime, it seemed.

"Clever Fauntleroy," approved Caroline now, patting him fondly. And Fauntleroy gave her a kindly smile and trotted off on some unspecified business of his own, followed determinedly by Chunky.

By this time the morning was wearing on. Aunt Amethyst had not returned, and the children decided to resume their exploring. The drawing-room fire and the dusting could wait. It would be better, Kit had suggested, to gain an over-all impression of the house first, so that they could get their bearings.

"Yes, well, let's try the doors on the *other* side of the hall," proposed Richard. "We've seen the drawing-room side and the back of the house. Now we ought to find out what's behind that heavy leather curtain. . . ."

"There's something about it . . . it looks mysterious," agreed Kit, touching with uncertain fingers the red leather *portière*.

"Well, here goes," said Richard—and he lifted it aside and revealed behind it another paneled oak door, similar to all the others.

They pushed it open, and found themselves in a long, low library, its walls masked from floor to ceiling with its book-lined shelves. On the left was a fireplace with a marble mantelpiece and in the three other walls were tall, deeply recessed windows with low, cushioned window seats and shutters that folded back against the paneling. By the hearth stood a large leather-covered armchair with a sagging seat, long since worn out by someone's weight; in the middle of the room was a round table of polished mahogany and against one of the windows stood a writing table, handsome and massive, of some pale golden wood, inlaid with a sort of dull green. The whole effect of the room was one of somber quietness; a strange, brooding, studious silence seemed to hang over it like a spell.

"Oh, books . . ." said Richard, disappointed.

"*Books!*" echoed Caroline, exultantly.

"Why, I've never *seen* so many books!" exclaimed Kit, quite awed.

As they stood there, looking around them, there was the sudden silvery chiming of a clock striking eleven, and this drew their attention to the mantelpiece. It was of black marble, and so was the clock. At each end of the mantelpiece stood a pair of old-fashioned glass lamps with small pendants that swung and tinkled at a touch; on one side of the clock was a mother-of-pearl snuffbox, and on the other a small object that might have escaped their close attention had not the sun shone out at that moment and, striking boldly through the opposite window, lit it up in a peculiar manner.

It was a small glass globe set on a black marble base, and inside it . . . Well, what *was* inside it?

"A house," said Richard, "with trees around." He lifted it carefully. "Crikey, it's heavy enough! I suppose it's a paperweight. . . . Gosh! What's happening?"

For white specks had suddenly started to whirl around the house, getting larger and larger till they almost hid it in a veritable snowstorm.

And, of course, that was just what it was.

"A *snowstorm!*" exclaimed Caroline, who had a toy one of her own at home, with Westminster Abbey inside it. "What a beauty! Let's take it to the window. . . ."

Chapter 3

THE SNOWSTORM

In the brilliance of morning sunshine after rain, the snowstorm, as its snowflakes subsided, was indeed revealed as a masterpiece of delicate precision. The stately gray house with its tall chimney stacks and gabled roofs, its paved courtyard and its stone terraces and steps leading down to sweeping lawns set with cedar trees, was as near perfection as anything could be. There was even a peacock on the terrace, and a little lake with swans.

"How *real* it looks," commented Kit. "You could almost fancy one of those windows opening and someone shaking out a duster."

"Or coming out of the front door," agreed Richard. "A boy, perhaps," he added wistfully.

All three children stared intently into the snowstorm,

and it was very odd but suddenly they each of them had the strangest sensation that they were, in fact, standing in front of this model house, staring up at its windows, that one of the windows was actually opening and a boy's face peering out— a dark-haired boy with a merry face and friendly eyes. . . . "Hello!" an excited voice hailed them. "Who are you?"

Not one of them dared say a word, so sure were they that they were dreaming. Then, suddenly, they were back in the library, looking at each other with startled eyes.

"Hello!" said an excited voice behind them, like the echo of a dream. "Who are you?"

And they turned around to find a boy of about Richard's age behind them, a dark boy with friendly eyes and a merry smile.

"My name's Michael," volunteered the stranger.

"Mine's Rick," returned Richard, and he spoke eagerly, for he was thinking to himself that this was indeed just exactly the sort of boy he had had in mind. "And these are my sisters," he added politely, "Caroline and Kit."

"Aunt Amethyst didn't tell us there were any other children here," spoke up Kit, puzzled. "*Do* you live here?"

"Of course," said the boy in surprise. "She didn't tell me *you* were coming, either." He sounded just as bewildered as Kit. "I wonder why not? I've longed for someone my own age. It has been so lonely, with only Mr. Allardyce . . . ."

"Mr. Allardyce?"

"The tutor. Are you to have lessons with us?"

"Oh! I hope not! We never thought of it," frowned Richard. "Mother said there was a school somewhere near. Co-ed. We expected to go to that when the term starts. We don't," went on Richard on a rising note of alarm, "want lessons during the holidays."

"Ah!" said M'chael darkly. "It's not what *we* want—I found that out long ago."

Just then there was the sound of a car grinding and spluttering up the drive, and Kit turned to the window. "I suppose it's Aunt Amethyst," she said. "Anyway, it's the car we came in last night."

They all watched the erratic course of the gray station wagon over the stones and fallen branches that littered the avenue. "I will say the old girl can drive," remarked Richard admiringly. He put the snowstorm back on the mantelpiece. "Does she ever take you to market with her, Michael?"

But there was no answer. And when the children turned around to find out why not, they discovered to their amazement that Michael had vanished.

For a moment they were all speechless with astonishment. Then, "I don't think he was real . . . there was something strange about him," said Caroline earnestly, after a while. "Did you notice his clothes?"

"What was wrong with them?" demanded Richard, who never did notice clothes, anyway.

"They were queer. Queer and old-fashioned. The sort of clothes boys wore a long time ago. But not now. Not since . . . since . . ." Caroline floundered. "I don't know since when," she had to confess.

"Well, *I* don't think he was real, either," Kit agreed

unexpectedly. "The way he was suddenly here, and then not here. Besides . . ." Her voice trailed off. (Not for worlds would she have the others know of that strange feeling she'd had of seeing the boy in the house in the snowstorm.)

"Yes," admitted Richard with knitted brow. It was very odd. . . . He mustn't let the girls know, of course, or they'd think he was crazy, but certainly he had seen that face in the snowstorm.

He picked it up again and looked intently at the gabled house in its terraced gardens; but the sun had gone in now, the glass no longer sparkled, and somehow the snowstorm seemed dull and lifeless and the house just an ordinary little piece of clever work.

"I vote we don't say anything to Aunt Amethyst just yet," he suggested at last.

"Well, she didn't say anything to *us*," pointed out Kit.

"We can wait and see if she does now," nodded Caroline.

Aunt Amethyst did not say anything about Michael but she had plenty to say about children who went off and left the dirty breakfast things on the table and none of the dish-washing done.

"We're truly sorry we forgot, Aunt Amethyst," apologized Kit earnestly, "but we *were* going to light a fire in the drawing room for you and it was only because we suddenly saw Fauntleroy coming up the avenue with a basket in his mouth that we didn't."

"Then," said Aunt Amethyst, throwing up her hands dramatically, "thank heaven for Fauntleroy, for that chimney has three birds' nests blocking it, and seven bricks and two cornerpieces have fallen in, and you'd have burned the whole place down."

The children went quite pale at the very thought of such a narrow escape and their aunt observed the fact with every satisfaction. "Never take anything in this house at its face value," said she, weightily, "and never forget for one minute that the poor old place is falling more deeply into ruin with every breath you take."

"Oh!" gasped the children, and they all simultaneously held their breath for a moment as if they could thus prevent the disaster.

"Tile by tile, brick by brick," continued Aunt Amethyst, warming to her subject, "the old place is falling . . . falling . . . like autumn leaves. Ah, it breaks my heart to say so, for I love every stick and stone of the old house and every single object in it. But that's the way things are, and what can a mere woman do about it? Dooley helps me patch up here and there—but Dooley is an old man, and I—I am a very old woman."

"You're *not*," whispered Caroline, but Aunt Amethyst did not hear her.

"Who is Dooley?" asked Richard.

"That is Dooley, out there in the garden. He lives near Mrs. Tidy and, like her, he bicycles in every day. I suppose you could call him a sort of general handyman."

Following their aunt's glance the children saw an old, bent man with a sack arranged over his shoulders like a cape and trousers tied tightly around the knee with string. He was sweeping leaves off the lawn and taking them away to a bonfire. "You'll meet him sometime.

Meanwhile, I'll wash and you can wipe and then—well, it's Mrs. Tidy's day off today, so we must see what we can rake up to eat."

Very familiar now sounded that ominous phrase, but by this time the children felt pretty sure that there was really nothing to worry about. There would always be something to eat at Farthingales, no matter how grim or uncertain Aunt Amethyst made the outlook seem.

And indeed it turned out that after lighting the fire that morning (and she never had a day off from *that,* it appeared) Mrs. Tidy, with admirable foresight, had popped into the oven before she left the two rabbits which had been on the back seat of the car the evening before (and from which Caroline and Kit had had the greatest difficulty in keeping Chunky) and there they were in the oven still, accounting for all the delicious savory odors that were beginning to fill the kitchen.

"And we'll have roast chestnuts and potatoes," beamed Aunt Amethyst happily. "What about sprouts—anyone like Brussels sprouts?"

In the bustle of preparing the delicious meal, the boy named Michael was almost forgotten. Almost, but not quite. At the backs of their minds the children were both excited and disturbed, burning to ask their aunt about him. Yet, at the same time, something, they knew not what, kept them silent as they had already agreed.

The midday meal having been duly disposed of, and all traces washed up and cleared away, the children thought they would like to explore outside.

"That's right," approved Aunt Amethyst. "You ought

to have some fresh air while the sun is out. Like as not it will be raining again tomorrow. But you'll have to go yourselves, I'm afraid. I'm busy this afternoon. Perhaps Dooley . . ."

Aunt Amethyst's voice trailed off uncertainly, but, the children assured her, they would much rather explore on their own. So off they went, with Chunky and Fauntleroy padding amiably behind. "Fauntleroy," said Aunt Amethyst, "will see you don't get lost."

"Get lost!" echoed Richard outside, in deep disdain. "How old does she think we are?"

Yet the remark was not really as foolish as it sounded, for everything in the garden was so overgrown and there were so many paths winding confusingly between high banks of rhododendrons and other tangled shrubs that it really was quite a task to keep one's bearings. Presently, however, they found themselves emerging onto wide lawns, one of them set with a small round lake and another with three immense cedar trees.

"They'll be good fun for climbing," Richard observed appreciatively, "and we could build a tree house up there, as easy as winking."

On the far side of the lawns, through a faded blue door in a wall which extended up to the house, they came upon the kitchen garden, and this indeed was as neat as could be, with its stone pigeon cote, its square box-edged plots packed full of fruit trees and bushes, vegetables and herbs. In one corner was a long glass house with a furnace, and deep tanks. A grapevine rambled along the roof and the children recalled their aunt saying, at suppertime last evening, that she took grapes to market in the summer, and tomatoes, and cut flowers.

"But just now it's only eggs and vegetables," recollected Kit, "and look—there are the chickens, over there."

She pointed through another open doorway in the brick wall to a long range of chicken houses standing in spacious runs in a meadow.

"No wonder it's eggs for breakfast every morning," commented Caroline.

After that they wandered around and found yet a third blue door, and this led them into the shrubbery again, where once more they missed their way. For now they could hear the river somewhere quite close at hand, without being able to discover quite where, and in their efforts to obey its calling voice they soon lost all sense of direction. Then Fauntleroy let them down and dashed off after a rabbit, followed enthusiastically by Chunky, and when at length the children came upon the river, chattering and laughing over its stony bed, they had no idea how to get back to the house again.

"Hush . . . hush . . . hush . . ." the river had murmured drowsily through Caroline's dreams the night before.

But there was nothing drowsy about it now. It raced and tumbled noisily over its stony shallows, pouring whitely over rocky ledges and swirling dizzily into little whirlpools. Presently they could hear the steady falling, falling sound of a waterfall somewhere higher up the river's course, and overgrown though the path was, they pushed their way through briar and bramble to find it. They slipped on mud and sloshed through puddles, the falling, falling sound becoming louder every minute and at last there it was, ahead of them, about ten or twelve feet of foaming water tumbling in a white cascade from a rocky ledge high above. Climbing up to this ledge by a flight of rough steps beside the waterfall, they found they had left the trees below them and were standing on a sort of grassy plateau, the rocky precipice and the cataract on one side and wide views over the moors on the other, with the sea shining blue and silver in the distance.

And it was then that they made their exciting discovery.

"Look!" cried Caroline, pointing down the way they had come. "There it is—there's Farthingales."

Yes, there it was, neat as a toy with its clustered outbuildings, its spreading gardens and orchards and stone pigeon cote. Moreover, there was something familiar about it—about those gables and tall chimney stacks, the terraces and the lawns set with cedar trees, and the little lake.

"Why, of course!" exclaimed Caroline. "We might have known! It's the house in the snowstorm!"

And so indeed it was.

Somehow or other the day ended without one single word having been said to Aunt Amethyst about Michael and their adventure in the library.

"It was just a feeling we had—that it was something we ought to keep to ourselves," Kit reflected as they went up to bed, leaving Aunt Amethyst busy with household accounts in the kitchen.

"And maybe we shouldn't have been *in* the library anyway," added Caroline. "There's something about it that's different from the other rooms—that red leather curtain is probably meant to keep us out."

"No, it's not," scoffed Richard. "It's only to ensure silence for whoever is trying to read. Still . . ."

Yes, *still*, there *was* something about the library. Something . . . *some*thing. . . . What *was* it?

"It's a feeling of things being *concentrated* there," said Kit, screwing up her forehead with the effort of thinking. "Something watchful, as if . . ."

"As if what?"

"I don't know," Kit had to confess.

Then Richard manfully came out with it, calmly and matter-of-factly. "Well, I do. It's my belief the library is haunted," he said bluntly.

There was a silence into which all sorts of little sounds dropped like pebbles—the ticking of the grandfather clock on the landing, the faint sound of the river far off, the tiny scamper of a mouse somewhere.

"Haunted? Who by?" whispered Caroline at last.

"Come off it. You know who," rebuked her brother severely.

"By Michael?"

"Yes."

So that was it! Yes . . . What else could explain it? Richard was right. The room *did* feel haunted. But not unpleasantly. Somehow you couldn't feel afraid—only excited.

"I don't know how it was, but I knew at once when I saw that red curtain that something was going to happen through that door," Caroline recollected.

"If only Michael hadn't disappeared so quickly," mused Kit. "I wonder what made him do that? Perhaps it was the noise of the car coming up the drive. Vibrations, or something. Or perhaps you have to keep your eyes on him all the time."

Perhaps . . . perhaps. . . . What a tiresome word that is!

"Well, let's try again tomorrow," suggested Richard sensibly. "I've an idea it's something to do with the snowstorm."

Ah, the snowstorm!

"Yes," agreed Caroline, hesitating. And then, in a burst of confidence, she added quickly, "You know, I first saw Michael *in* the snowstorm. I was in it myself, somehow."

"Me, too," nodded Kit quietly. "I was in it as well, and Michael was looking down on us from one of the windows."

Richard caught his breath. "Yes, I was there, too. *I* saw him."

So that was the answer! The snowstorm!

"Tomorrow, then, we'll try again," repeated Richard firmly.

Tomorrow . . . ! Would it *never* come? Caroline lay awake and looked at the Hundred Eyes and wondered if Michael had once done the same thing. Who was he? What was it that brought him back to the library? There must be *something*.

In the next room Richard was pondering the same question. "If only he were real he could be my pal. We could have adventures together." Then he thought, "Well, for the few moments he's with us he *is* real. It's because we believe in him. And if we go *on* believing . . ."

He sat up in bed excitedly. He was on the track of something big and deep. . . . "If we *go on* believing in him he'll *go on* being real, alive!"

It was a stupendous thought, but too big for him quite to grasp. It made his head swim. "Perhaps tomorrow . . ." he thought sleepily. "T'morrow. . . ."

Chapter 4

RUMMAGE IN THE ATTICS

And at last tomorrow came—another wet day—and in the meantime Aunt Amethyst had had a bright idea. She wanted the children to help her turn out rummage from the attics for the Boy Scouts.

Now yesterday they would have jumped at it. Yesterday, as you may remember, Richard had remarked with enthusiasm that there must be a lot of rummage at Farthingales.

But today it all seemed rather tiresome. Perversely, they wanted Aunt Amethyst to go out again and leave them to their own devices—and Aunt Amethyst, it seemed, had no intention of doing any such obliging thing.

Well, it couldn't be helped. And the attics might turn

out to be quite interesting. At least it would be a new experience.

"I've never been in an attic before," confided Caroline as they went upstairs.

"Haven't you, child? Dusty places, mostly. Drafty, too, and can be damp, sometimes, when tiles are missing. But on the whole I enjoy rummaging up here. Never know what you may come upon."

"Old jewels hidden away?" suggested Caroline tentatively. "Valuable pictures under piles of rubbish?"

Aunt Amethyst gave a hoot of laughter. "Anything of that sort was unearthed and sold years ago—you can bet your Sunday boots on *that*. But it's something if I find another old overall with some wear in it, or a plaid shawl, or a waterproof cape for Dooley to wear in the garden. Quite apart, of course, from what we find for the Scouts."

The attics at Farthingales constituted quite a world of their own. As the children reached the top of the rickety twisting stairway leading up to them and followed their aunt into the first one, they found that they could see from this end of the house to the other. The whole dusty shadowy region, with its series of intercommunicating garrets on different levels, lit only by skylights and tiny dormer windows, would be ideal, they thought, for hide-and-seek. There was a swing attached to one of the beams, too, and an old gray rocking horse, rearing ghostly with every draught, for it was here, Aunt Amethyst told them, that generations of Faraday children had been sent up to play on wet days. In another attic were rows and rows of apples laid out on the floor. "Cox's Orange and a few

Blenheims. And the mice have started on them already, I see. The little beggars certainly know when they're onto a good thing," Aunt Amethyst remarked.

" 'At the top of the house the apples are laid in rows,' " murmured Caroline dreamily.

"What's that, child?"

"Nothing. Just a poem we learned at school. . . .

And the skylight lets the moonlight in, and those
Apples are deep-sea apples of green. There goes
A cloud on the moon in the autumn night.

"I love it. . . ."

"So do I. I'm glad you know your Drinkwater."

A mouse in the wainscot scratches and scratches and then
There is no sound at the top of the house of men. . . .

"It perfectly catches Farthingales, doesn't it?" Aunt Amethyst flashed her a smile. "Well, we must get on. *Tempus fugit.*"

She opened a trunk and they found old lesson books, a box of dominoes, snakes-and-ladders, a pair of old letter-scales, a discarded radio. "Hmmm. It looks almost as good as the one I use," commented Aunt Amethyst, looking doubtfully at this last item. "Still, they can have it. Put everything in this box and we'll see what else we can find."

Another trunk yielded china ornaments. Kit said she really couldn't imagine anyone wanting them, for most of them were just hideous, but Aunt Amethyst assured her she had absolutely no idea what strange things people bought at rummage sales. "Somewhere I've got an old pair of Wellington boots. Now they would be useful to someone. They're too small for Dooley and too big for me. I wonder where they've gone?"

Just then Fauntleroy suddenly set up an urgent barking downstairs. Aunt Amethyst looked at her watch. "Ah, that would be the piano tuner. Come and take these things from me, Kit, and look for the Wellington boots while I go down, will you, children? Here's my flashlight. I'll be back presently."

She dusted her hands hastily on her apron and endeavored to smooth down her hair but, even as she turned to go, there was a scampering sound on the stairs and Fauntleroy appeared impatiently in the doorway with the piano tuner's card. "All right, I'm coming, lad," she called, apologetically. "Good man!" And Aunt Amethyst disappeared obediently.

"Wellingtons, eh?" commented Richard. "Well, where should we look for anything like that? Not in a trunk."

"Most likely they'd be in a closet, or standing in a corner," agreed Kit.

They looked around the vast, dusty place, and certainly there seemed to be enough closets. The problem was—which one?"

"We'll have to look in them all," observed Richard, not without pleasure; for there is something exciting about a closet, especially in an attic, and who knew what, besides Wellingtons, they might come across?

"Well, this one is empty," reported Kit, straightening herself up from a sort of locker under a dormer window.

"Only cobwebs in this one, too," nodded Caroline, who

had found a little closet in a chimney stack.

"This one's better, though. Lots of stuff here," called Richard cheerfully, moving his flashlight around. He had found a long low cupboard enclosing the space where the ceiling rafters sloped down to the floor, and inside were things like rusty fire irons, a broken saddle, an old bird-cage, and goodness knows what else. "Everything in the world except Wellingtons," as Kit remarked.

They went into the next attic and found other closets, but these, too, seemed to be mostly empty, except for one which on closer inspection was found to contain a broken footstool and an old black cape hanging from a peg.

"I reckon they must be in one of the trunks, after all," said Caroline. "Let's start with the biggest, and then . . . Why, Rick, what's the matter?"

Richard's face was alight with excitement. "Look! See here!"

With some idea that the long black cape might be just the sort of thing that Aunt Amethyst wanted for Dooley, he had lifted it down from its peg. It was stiff and rotten with age, however, so that it almost fell to pieces in his hands, and behind it . . . behind it was revealed a low door, standing slightly ajar. It was only a few feet high —in fact it reminded Caroline of the little door through which Alice found the bottle labeled "Drink Me"—and beyond it a flight of dusty stairs twisted down, down, down into darkness.

"My word!" exclaimed Kit, craning her neck to see more clearly. "If that isn't great!"

"Can't have been used for years," observed Richard, trying to speak calmly. "The dust is inches thick and there aren't any footprints in it."

"There soon will be, though," said Kit determinedly. "You don't find secret stairways and not explore them. What a good thing we've got the flashlight."

"But . . ." demurred Caroline anxiously, "how do we know . . . I mean, it may not be safe. The stairs may be rotten."

"Rubbish! Don't be a spoilsport, Caro. Come on, Rick, I'll go first, if you like."

"You won't, then." Richard stepped down smartly. "The steps are stone, anyway, Caroline, so you needn't worry." He explored with the flashlight carefully. "Block the door with that old footstool so that it can't close after us—it seems stiff but it *might,* if there were drafts. . . ."

Within a few seconds they were all three of them creeping cautiously down the stone stairway. The dust muffled their footsteps and got into their noses and made them sneeze. Now and then they felt a draft of air from somewhere, but there was no gleam of light. The stairs were evidently built into the thickness of the wall and the torch revealed nothing else ahead of them. The steps themselves were narrow and fairly steep: they had to be descended with caution.

"Do be careful, Rick, won't you," Caroline said rather shakily. "It's so horribly dark, and if you drop the flashlight . . ."

"Well, I *shan't* drop it," Richard replied irritably. "You'd better go back, Caro, if you're scared."

"I'm not. And I couldn't go back, anyway—there's no room to turn around."

That was true enough. "So there's nothing to do but

to keep on keeping on," said Kit sensibly. "Cheer up, Caroline! We'll soon be there. And where's 'there?' "

Where indeed!

Suddenly Caroline forgot her fears in the excitement of the adventure. After all, she thought presently, as she plodded gamely on after the others, down, down, down . . . after all, it couldn't be much farther now.

". . . Thirty-two . . . thirty-three . . ." muttered Richard, who had been counting all the time. "Look out, kids, there's a broken step here . . . thirty-four . . . thirty-five . . . Gosh! I believe that's the lot!"

It was true. There were no more steps; instead they were confronted by a door with a latch. It was harsh and rusty to the touch, that latch, but "It's all right!" Richard called up excitedly. "It's lifting!" Yes, and the door was opening! A burst of light flooded gloriously into the dusty darkness. The children stepped forward and found themselves in the library!

"Of all that's wonderful!" exclaimed Kit.

"Smart piece of work," agreed Richard, grinning.

"Magic!" whispered Caroline, too enormously relieved to be out of the dark to think of anything else.

Richard examined the door. There was no latch or handle on this side. It was not so much a door as a section of the bookshelves—"And it looks as if it fits in invisibly with the rest, doesn't it?" he said. He pushed it back carefully and found that he was right. In fact, it glided into position as easily as if it were oiled: there was a click—and nobody would have known there was a door there at all. Nor did there appear to be any way of opening it again.

"Well, that's that, then," said Kit. "Sort of one-way-traffic idea."

"Thank goodness, too," smiled Caroline, thankful that there could be no question of returning to the attics by the same route. "And while we're here . . ."

"Yes," agreed Richard. "While we're here we'll see if Michael's about."

He took up the snowstorm. It looked just ordinary, but then perhaps there had to be a period of waiting? They all gathered round and stared into it, hard. But it remained just exactly what it was—a paperweight. No more.

"Let's take it to the window," suggested Caroline. "Perhaps it needs a clearer light."

So they took it to the window. But even the clearer light couldn't alter the fact that it was just . . . what it was.

"If only the sun would come out!" cried Kit in disappointment.

But there was no sign of the sun. In fact, it was still raining.

They took the snowstorm back to the mantelpiece and looked at each other glumly. "Guess we've had it," said Richard. "We'd better get upstairs again and find those Wellingtons."

Out in the hall they could hear the piano tuner running up and down the scales, striking imposing chords and bursting out into gay little snatches of melody. The door opened as they stood listening and Aunt Amethyst came out. She did not look in the least surprised to see them there.

"Ah, children! So you've come down. Good. I've just remembered that I gave the Wellingtons to Mrs. Tidy's nephew."

Chapter 5

MICHAEL

By the time the piano tuner had gone the children had been up to the attics again and brought down the box of rummage for the Scouts.

"Come into the drawing room," called Aunt Amethyst through the open door as they came downstairs. "Does anyone in these benighted days of radio and television know how to play the piano?"

"Kit does!" exclaimed Caroline eagerly.

"Yes, I do!" confirmed Kit, hardly daring to breathe.

"Then come and play to me, child. Play what you like. Whatever it is, it will be balm to one who feared that the piano was fast becoming as dead as the dodo."

Kit sat down on the long tapestried stool, and her hands trembled a little in her excitement. Then she started to play *"Le Petit Âne Blanc."*

Alas, before long her fingers stumbled; her memory had failed her. "The Little White Donkey can't finish his journey today," apologized Kit at last, and after a pause she embarked upon Handel's slow and stately minuet from *Berenice* instead.

Alas, again, even *Berenice* escaped her—perhaps it was the grandeur of the grand piano?—and before long Kit's hands fell into her lap once more in despair.

"Don't give up, Kit," urged Caroline. "Try you-know-what."

And Kit shot her a glance of gratitude and, as if suddenly inspired, swept swiftly and amazingly into Chopin's *Fantaisie Impromptu.* It was her favorite; she knew it by heart, and because they had the record at home, she knew exactly how it should be played.

The audience sat around in the faded, dusty drawing room and listened in silence.

"Why, you're a marvel, child!" cried Aunt Amethyst, when at length the last notes echoed into silence. "Playing from memory, too. Do you know who you get that from? You get it from *me!* It's a Faraday trick." She got up and went to the piano. "Have you had lessons?"

Kit shook her head. "I've just taught myself from Mother's books, and played whatever I felt like—or tried to! I've certainly never had lessons."

"I thought not," nodded Aunt Amethyst in satisfaction. "Like me, again. And music lessons cost money. Well, you *shall* have them, child, right now—from the only person who can teach you—me! When we've had something to eat, that is," she added reassuringly.

Caroline and Richard looked relieved, even Kit smiled, and a general exit was made, *en route* for the kitchen.

That afternoon, true to her word, Aunt Amethyst shepherded Kit into the drawing room. It was quite warm by the piano, for she had left there the blue oil stove with the slatted top which had been brought in for the piano tuner's benefit. "I can't spare you more than half an hour," she said, "but we can accomplish quite a lot in that time. Meanwhile, you two can amuse yourselves elsewhere, can't you?" It was more a statement than a question, and in fact she had firmly closed the drawing-room door before they could answer.

"I'll say we can," agreed Richard succinctly. "Come on, Caro." And the two of them made for the library like arrows shot from a bow.

The sun had come out an hour or two before, and it was streaming into the room now in a veritable tide of gold. Richard picked up the paperweight and took it to the window. Caroline followed him and they stared into it together. It had its special look, as if it shone. Every window in the house seemed to gleam with gold; as they looked it seemed to grow larger, to loom up above them, and—yes, there was Michael, at the library window. He was looking straight at them, and smiling.

"Hello, Michael," said Caroline quickly, before he could vanish.

The boy in the snowstorm seemed to grow larger; that queer sense of the house towering up above them faded away, and, all at once, the boy in the snowstorm had become the boy in the library.

"Hello," smiled back Michael gravely, "I hoped I'd find you here."

"So did we," nodded Richard.

"What's that you have in your hand?" added Michael curiously. "Why," he exclaimed excitedly, "it's my paper-weight!"

"The snowstorm," nodded Richard, shaking it up vigorously and setting a white blizzard raging.

"Is it yours, then?" inquired Caroline.

"Yes . . ." Michael's eyes shone. "You mustn't breathe a word to Grandfather, or my aunt, or to Mr. Allardyce, but it has magic powers. I can't explain it, but if you stare into it, if you utterly *lose* yourself in it, you will find you can step back into other times. I think perhaps it is really a sort of crystal, with the power of revealing the past, present, and future."

"But it can't be," protested Richard. "A crystal would be solid. This is just a hollow shell of glass, enclosing the model of the house. I know how they're made—I saw the sort of thing at the glassworks we visited last term at school."

"Yet there *may* be some element of crystals about it," persisted Michael. "Something . . . somewhere . . . I don't know what. Perhaps the house itself is made of crystal?"

Richard looked closely at it, at the fine detail and the exquisite modeling. "I couldn't say—I don't know enough about it. But I suppose it *might* be. As for the glass globe enclosing it—well, even just plain glass is funny stuff."

"*Wonderful* stuff," corrected Caroline gravely. "The things it can do—reflecting, magnifying . . ."

"Bending light rays and throwing them back," agreed Richard, warming to the thought.

"And splitting them up into all the colors of the rainbow," his sister reminded him.

"Prisms," nodded Richard. "Yes . . . They told us at the glassworks that there can even be reflections *inside* glass when it's in the form of a prism. That's why they're used in the periscopes of submarines." He looked thoughtfully at the snowstorm. "Yes, you're right, Caro. Glass *is* wonderful. Prisms and lenses . . . optical glass . . . you can do anything with it."

"It could be, then, that Michael is somehow on the right track?" ventured Caroline. "Just imagine a crystal, having the powers Michael spoke of, inside glass—and not ordinary glass, either—a special kind. Optical glass, perhaps—if it could be cast in such a mold?"

"Optical?" repeated Michael. "That means . . . ?"

"Having to do with optics; seeing," said Caroline. She spied a dictionary on the round table in the middle of the room and quickly looked up the word for Michael's benefit. "See, here we are: optics—'The science of the nature and laws of vision and light.'" Somehow they all felt very important and learned and on the verge of great discoveries.

"But would optical glass have been discovered in the days when this snowstorm was made?" said Richard half to himself.

Michael looked puzzled, but Caroline answered him quickly. "It could have been. Don't you remember how you had to read up about all the new processes for making optical glass that scientists found during the last century?

About Sir Humphrey Davy and John Dollond and Michael Faraday . . ." And suddenly Caroline broke off, her cheeks aflame with excitement. "Why—what a co-incidence! *Michael Faraday!*" she echoed.

And Michael smiled. "Yes, I have been learning about him too. But it's not exactly a coincidence. We're not kinsmen, but I was named after him. My grandfather knows him. So did my father."

"But how odd!" exclaimed Caroline. "It may be a clue, though. It may be that the someone who named you after him—your father?—was interested in science and physics?"

Michael nodded. "He was—my grandfather *and* my great-grandfather."

"Then it seems to me, Michael," said Richard, "that this snowstorm with Farthingales inside it could actually have been *made* by someone in the family. Someone who was interested in glass, experimented with it. Perhaps even manufactured it."

"And perhaps, quite by accident, produced something that had magic powers . . . he may not even have *known* it had them," reflected Michael.

"How did *you* first discover it?" asked Richard.

"I was busy with my studies," recollected Michael. "It was summer and the window was open and the breeze kept on blowing my papers to the floor. As I reached for the paperweight I shook it up and set the snowstorm going, and suddenly, all at once, I was *in* the snowstorm and there were children snowballing. They wore gar-ments worn in the time of the great Queen Elizabeth—cloaks and bonnets, doublets and hose, leather jerkins, and such like. There were three girls and a boy. One little girl had golden hair—she wore a blue cloak, and she was the fastest of them all. . . . I had one of her snowballs down my neck," recalled Michael with some resentment. "Yet, I tell you, it was *summer*—it was *June!*"

"Yes . . . It's magic," whispered Caroline. "*Whatever* the snowstorm is made of. And probably we'll never be able to explain it—because, you see, you *can't* explain magic. It wouldn't *be* magic if you could."

They all fell silent for a while, turning over in their minds the strange story. And then suddenly the sound of music filtered into the room: Handel's *Berenice*.

"Listen," said Michael, smiling, "Mr. Allardyce."

"It isn't," Caroline started to say. "It's Kit."

But the words died on her lips, for, surprisingly, Michael was making for the door. Richard and Caroline exchanged glances. Don't say a thing! Richard's face said—and the two of them followed their friend without a word.

"Poor Mr. Allardyce," said Michael gently, pushing aside the red leather *portière* and crossing the hall.

"Poor?" queried Caroline.

"Yes," answered Michael, but did not offer to explain himself. He turned the handle of the drawing-room door and Caroline uttered a stifled exclamation and grasped Richard's hand.

For the room was bright with color; a fire leaped and crackled on the stone hearth. There was no Kit, no Aunt Amethyst, no blue oil stove. But there at the piano sat someone who certainly could only be Mr. Allardyce: a

tall, gentle-looking young man with curly brown hair.
He wore a black suit, of a strange, old-fashioned cut—
even as Michael's was—and a white tie. He looked up
as they came in, and he smiled, but did not speak, just
went on playing quietly, almost as if to himself.

Then, above the gentle music, a querulous old voice
demanded, "Is that you, Michael?" and from a deep wing
armchair standing with its back toward them beside the
hearth, a gnarled old hand was held out.

"Yes, Grandfather, it is I," said Michael, going around
to the front of the chair. "How are you today, sir?"

"Ah, middling fair, boy, middling fair. Have you
finished your lessons?"

"Yes. And I've brought my new cousins to see you."

Grandfather Faraday surveyed the children without
much interest and they in turn surveyed him with a great
deal. He was a white-haired old man with shaggy eye-
brows over piercingly keen, dark blue eyes. He wore a
black-velvet skullcap and a sort of frilly cravat or stock
at the neck, but the rest of his apparel was hidden under
a plaid rug. "The drawing room is very apt to get chilly,
and Grandfather has not been well," explained Michael
in a whisper. "He may not say much to you—he really
does not do much except sleep these days."

"Pleased to meet you," Michael's grandfather was
muttering vaguely at the same time. "Pleased to meet
you, I'm sure. I don't know which of the twelve you
belong to, or where you've come from, but you're welcome." And he closed his eyes and went to sleep.

"What does he mean—which of the twelve?" asked
Caroline.

"Well, he had twelve children—didn't you know? My father was one of them, and Aunt Amethyst is the youngest. The twelfth child is always called Amethyst when it's a girl—it's a sort of Faraday tradition. 'The twelfth an amethyst,' you know."

"It's in the Bible," nodded Richard.

"Revelations," supplemented Caroline. "The pearly gates."

"Yes. Well, there were Timothy, Adam, Esther, and Paul. Then came Candace, Ruth, Daniel, and John. Lastly there were Damaris, James, Mark, and Amethyst."

"All out of the Bible, every one," observed Caroline.

"Yes. Well, which of them *do* you belong to?" demanded Michael impatiently.

Caroline and Richard exchanged anxious glances.

"We . . . Well, we don't belong to any of them, I'm afraid. Our mother's name is Lucy."

Michael nodded slowly. "I see how it is," he said in a low voice. "It's as I feared . . . you're not my cousins, really. . . . It's the snowstorm . . . you're out of the *future*. That explains your queer clothes."

"Yes," admitted Richard guardedly. "Well . . ."

"Well . . ." demurred Caroline uneasily.

"Well, I think it is simply *wonderful!*" concluded Michael.

Richard and Caroline let out audible sighs of relief.

"Yes, it *is* wonderful," agreed Caroline eagerly. "Through the snowstorm, it seems, we have the run of time. We haven't told Aunt Amethyst yet," she added, "but she would love to hear about it. She loves Farthingales—every stick and stone of it. How thrilled she'd be to see you—and all this." She waved her hand around the beautiful room. "I suppose you don't know of any hidden treasure knocking about, Michael, or something like that? Something that would help her to live an easier life? She has to work so hard, poor dear—but she'd sooner starve than leave the old place."

"Of course she would—she couldn't do it," agreed Michael, shocked. "She's a Faraday of Farthingales."

"Yes. Maybe she is. But these times we live in are hard, Michael. Not like in your day. The house is falling into ruin and there are things like taxes and death duties, for instance, that eat up the money. And then, you see, people can't afford to keep large staffs nowadays, either indoors or out, so they have to shut up the best part of their houses and live in a few of its rooms. Like Aunt Amethyst. There's only Mrs. Tidy to help her indoors, and Dooley out. Mrs. Burbage, the housekeeper, wouldn't stay—Aunt Amethyst couldn't afford her wages."

"Mrs. Burbage . . . Oh, I know *her*," said Michael. "Aunt Amethyst goes down to the village to see her sometimes—she had to give up her work here. She has a ne'er-do-well husband. He never works and he never washes or has his hair cut. The village children have a song about him—something about 'Old Gaffer Burbage, covered in herbage.' "

"Poor old boy," grinned Richard.

"Of course, though, that is an earlier Mrs. Burbage," reminded Caroline gently. "Not ours. And *your* Aunt Amethyst, not ours."

"Yes. Tell me about yours. Is she pretty, like mine?"

"We haven't seen yours yet. But—yes, she's pretty.

When she has time she can look absolutely fab. But it's nearly all work, so she's mostly dressed in breeches and an old windbreaker." Caroline paused, and added wistfully, "That's why I said . . . that's why I asked . . . You haven't heard of any . . . any . . ."

"Hidden treasure? No. But Grandfather might, perhaps."

"What's that about hidden treasure?" demanded a cracked voice from the armchair. The old gentleman had awakened and was fixing them with a piercing blue gaze. Mr. Allardyce stopped playing for a moment and stared at them, too.

"*Is* there any at Farthingales, sir?" asked Michael.

"If there were, I wouldn't tell you," replied the old man cantankerously. "Hidden treasure, indeed! Nonetheless," he muttered, "Farthingales has its secrets." And he went off to sleep again.

"Secrets!" echoed Richard. "By golly, yes! I'll bet it has!" He suddenly remembered the morning's adventure. "Did you know that there's a sort of secret passage from the library up into the attics, Michael?"

"Yes. My aunt told me. In the old days mass had to be held in secret in the attics, you know."

"M'mmmm." Caroline had been looking thoughtful. Now she changed the subject. "You know, even if there isn't any treasure in the exciting sense of the word, I'm sure there are any amount of *household* treasures here that Aunt Amethyst could *sell*."

Michael looked severe. "Possibly they've been repossessed."

"They've not. Aunt Amethyst says that everything

valuable has gone, but there are lots of *wonderful* things in the house still. Kit and I sleep in a Tudor four-poster bed, for instance, twined with Tudor roses, and then there are Restoration chairs, with crowns carved on the backs, and a marvelous Chinese lacquer cabinet. They *are* valuable—it's just that she doesn't want to part with them."

"Of course not. She wouldn't. She's a F . . ."

"Faraday of Farthingales?" chorused the children blithely.

"Yes, well, that's what I mean. Faradays don't sell their inheritance."

"But it may come to it yet. What good would all those things be without Farthingales itself? And if the old house is going to fall into ruin for want of a bit of money . . ."

"Yes, it's a difficult problem," conceded Michael.

"What is a difficult problem?" came Grandfather Faraday's fretful voice again. "You children are worse than the starlings with your chatter. I cannot hear myself think." He twisted around testily in his chair. "Allardyce, I'm tired of Handel—let me have some Haydn for a change."

Mr. Allardyce reached for some music that lay on a small table nearby, but he was not quite near enough and it would have fallen to the floor had he not jumped up swiftly to save it. As he did so, his sudden clumsy movement overturned the stool he had been sitting on. It crashed against the wall with a noise like thunder and the echoes reverberated around the room in waves of vibration.

Suddenly, though no one was playing, there was the sound of music again, and all at once Caroline and Richard realized with a shock of dismay and disappointment that the scene had changed. Michael, his grandfather, Mr. Allardyce, the old-fashioned, square semigrand piano—all had vanished. The long drawing room was faded and dusty again. There was no fire, just the blue oil stove with the slatted top beside the ordinary present-day grand piano, and Kit and Aunt Amethyst at the keyboard, busy with their Handel.

"So," said Caroline to her sister in bed that night, "we thought we'd stay and listen to you. You're sure you and Aunt Amethyst were in the drawing room all the time? Right up to the moment you saw us standing there?"

"Every minute," affirmed Kit positively, "and to tell you the truth I was rather annoyed to see you. I'd been hoping that Aunt Amethyst would forget she had said she could only spare half an hour. I think she would have done it, too, and then you had to come in and spoil it all."

"We didn't mean to," apologized Caroline, "but all the same," she added, her mind going back over the events of the meeting with Michael and all that had followed, "you must have had well over half an hour. Why, you must have had almost the whole afternoon!"

"Indeed we didn't," denied Kit indignantly. "I had my watch, and it was half an hour to the minute when you came in."

"Well, I suppose it's the same sort of thing as dreaming," reflected Caroline. "You know, when you seem to

have been dreaming for hours and hours and it wasn't
five minutes even. . . . Time is different in other—in
differing—oh, I can't think of the word. . . ."

"On differing planes?"

"Yes, I suppose that's what I mean."

The two sisters were silent for a while. "I do wish I'd
been there," said Kit at length, impulsively. "Why did it
have to happen while I was having my lesson? Tell me
the whole thing again, Caro."

And, without regret, Caroline did.

Chapter 6

IN THE COACHHOUSE

The following day was bright and sunny and much colder. There had been a frost in the night and everything that could sparkle sparkled.

"You want to do something to warm yourselves up this morning," observed Aunt Amethyst at breakfast-time. "A walk to the village, perhaps, or a game of football. Or what about chopping me some wood? It's just the thing for setting the circulation going."

The children were not keen on the idea of football, and the village was so far away—nearly five miles. So in the end it was the last suggestion that won. As Kit remarked, there is something oddly satisfying about chopping wood. Lots of people have the same feeling. Maybe it is just the primitive urge toward destruction (this was Richard's contribution, and he was proud of this subtle bit of psychology), but Aunt Amethyst said that for her part it was the feeling of getting something for nothing. "Firewood costs money, but here at Farthingales there's enough old timber in one form or another to last for hundreds of years, maybe even centuries," she beamed happily.

Then she took them out to the coachhouse (it was still called the coachhouse even though there had been no coaches in it for a good fifty or sixty years) and left them to it.

Now it would not be true to say that the children had never chopped wood before, but they were certainly not experts, and before very long Richard had sliced off a piece of thumb and Kit had dropped the heavy chopper on her foot. By the time those mishaps occurred, however, they had managed to split up a big boxful of sticks, so Richard, wrapping his handkerchief around his scarlet-dripping thumb, suggested that they pack up for the time being and go exploring to take their minds off their injuries.

"That stairway up the wall looks interesting," he suggested.

It was a flight of stone stairs built against the wall and leading up to a sort of loft at one end of the long coachhouse. It had no handrail and the steps were not very wide, so Caroline, who had no head for heights, stayed down below while the other two went up, with Chunky following gamely after.

"No one can have been up here for years," observed Richard, "judging by the dust."

It was, indeed, inches thick, just as it had been on the attic stairs, as Kit commented. At the top they found themselves in what might at one time perhaps have been used as a granary, for there were a number of ancient sacks ranged against the wall. One had burst its seams and a heap of mildewy grain was strewn over the floor. A quantity of heavy lumber, trunks, and old furniture took up the rest of the space. Over it all was that same gray pall of cobwebby dust, muffling their footsteps and flying up as they disturbed it and getting into their throats. As they stood looking around them there was a faint scuttling sound in one corner, and Chunky, immediately on the alert, spied a rat and darted after it.

"Look at this," said Richard, poking about in the dust. "It's a musical box. Whoever heard of a musical box in a coachhouse loft?"

"Well, people get tired of things," pointed out Kit wisely, "and it's a job to know what to do with them. I imagine it's broken, anyway. Isn't it a beauty, though?" She looked admiringly at the gay picture of kittens and roses on the lid and rubbed her sleeve over it. "See, it only needs to be cleaned up—now let's find out if it will play."

Kit turned the handle, fully expecting to find it broken. But after a sort of preliminary hiccup it moved around quite easily and tinkled out "The Bluebells of Scotland."

Richard whistled appreciatively. "Great! Now let's see what else we can find."

But alas, in that tiresome manner in which things *do* let you down when you've become thoroughly excited, there really didn't seem to be anything else—just a dusty, dirty, chaotic jumble of worm-eaten old chests and flyblown mirrors all piled precariously on top of each other.

"We could look in the chests," suggested Kit.

"So we could," agreed Richard, starting forward.

Just then, however, their attention was suddenly drawn to Chunky, who had come trotting up behind them again, having apparently abandoned his rat. He was trying to shake himself free of the cobwebs that had plastered themselves over his eyes and nose. Then, all at once, he paused and stiffened. Kit and Richard looked all around in surprise, but there was nothing to be seen. "What's the matter, boy?" asked Richard sympathetically.

But Chunky backed away with a low growl, cowed and shaking as they had never seen him before. Suddenly he flinched and threw back his head, howling. Then, with his tail between his legs, he dragged himself along the floor to the steps. Down the steep stairway he scuttled and shot out into the sunshine as if jet-propelled.

"What on earth can have happened?" cried Kit, distressed. "Why, I've never seen him like that before."

Caroline was standing at the foot of the stone steps looking up at them with a strained, white face. "Oh, *do* come down," she begged.

"Oh, Caro!" exclaimed Richard. "You, too? What's come over everyone?"

Caroline shuddered. "Oh, he was a *horrible* old man! Didn't you see him? He was behind you all the time."

"An old man? There wasn't anyone up there besides us."

"But I'm *telling* you—there *was*. This old man—
Chunky must have seen him, too."

Well, it was perfectly obvious that Chunky had seen
something, so how could Kit and Richard argue? Still, it
was queer. "Where could he have come from, and where
did he go?" demanded Kit. "Don't you think perhaps you
saw Dooley? Maybe he keeps tools or something up
there."

"Oh, don't be *silly*, Kit. I've *seen* Dooley. It wasn't
him. It was someone with horribly long, matted hair and
a dirty beard, dressed in peculiar clothes. It looked as if
he hadn't washed or shaved for years. . . ." And suddenly
Caroline broke off. She seemed to hear Michael's voice:
*He never worked, he never washed, he never had his hair
cut.* . . . "Why, I do believe—I think it must have been
old Burbage," she whispered.

Richard whistled. "Old Gaffer Burbage, covered in
herbage. Gosh, Caro—in that case . . ."

Caroline nodded. "I know. That would be why you
couldn't see him. No wonder Chunky bolted. . . ."

Richard looked at her speculatively. "It's odd that you
should have seen him—you must have the sight, as they
call it."

Kit suddenly shivered. "What on earth are you two
talking about? I don't like this place. Let's get out into
the sunshine," she urged.

Outside, in the sheltered angle formed by the coachhouse and an adjoining barn, the January sun felt as
warm as June. They stood there a little while, basking in
it and talking in low voices of the strange occurrence,
and presently the trundle of a wheelbarrow sounded and

there was Dooley, smiling at them respectfully and saying good morning. The children looked at him sus-
piciously, but nothing cleaner, neater, and more whole-
some than Dooley's sturdy person could be imagined.

"You be the young master and missies as have come to
look after Miss Faraday," commented Dooley in a well-
informed manner. "I see'd ye yessiday when ye went
through my kitching garden. Ye didn't see me but I was
in my little shed by the large glasshouse. I be main
glad ye've come, my dears. Your aunt can do with young
folks like ye, and that's a truth. Lonesome like it be for
her here, with her dad gone and all them sarvants walkin'
out on her, the varmints. Like rats leavin' a sinkin' ship,
that's what it be."

The children nodded. "Except that the ship isn't going
to sink," said Richard firmly.

"No, I'll lay it won't, not with you three at the helm."
Dooley spoke with flattering certainty. "We'll keep
afloat, sarvants or no sarvants."

"Walked out, did they?" queried Kit.

"Aye, they did that." A glint of angry scorn came
into the old man's mild blue eyes. "Call 'emselves
sarvants! Can't exist, they can't, without a TV in the
housekeeper's room, and the electric light blazing from
every corner. Be wantin' hot 'n' cold in their bedrooms
next, they will. Spoonfed, that's what they be." The old
man took a pipe from his pocket and started filling it.
"Now, take *me*—I could have gone after the big money,
too. I worked my way up from gardener's boy to second
of four, and I'd hoped one day to be head, but World
War II put an end to that, it did. So here I am—doin'

what? Odd jobs. And by gum, I'll go *on* doin' 'em—for
Miss Amethyst."

The children looked impressed. "Of course, there's
Mrs. Tidy," said Caroline tentatively. "But it's not really
quite the same as having Mrs. Burbage always there,
Aunt Amethyst says."

"Ah, Mrs. Tidy! Now *she's* a proper bit of all right."
Dooley nodded his appreciation. "But that there Mrs.
Burbage—*no*. Miss Faraday be better off without her,
that she be. No good ever came out of them Burbages."

The children exchanged glances. "Is that so?" said
Richard politely.

"Insolent and lazy and a lot of thievin' magpies to
boot," confirmed Dooley, with a thunderous brow. "The
first one of 'em, old Jasper Burbage, he was hired for Sir
William Faraday at a giglet fair. No good ever came out
of hirin'."

"A giglet fair?" echoed Caroline.

"Aye. It was a fair they used to hold in them olden
days, mostly at Martinmas. The girls and young men,
they used to stand in rows in the market square to be
looked over for choosing. They wore colored ribbons
accordin' to what they was. A carter, he'd have a tuft of
white ribbon in his hat, a cook might wear a red 'un, and
a servin' maid a blue 'un. . . . No, it's as I say—no good
ever came out of hirin'—never knew who ye were
gettin.' Well, that was more'n a hunnerd an' fifty years
ago, I reckon—an' there've been Burbages about ever
since, an' more's the pity."

"What was he like, that first Burbage?" asked Richard
hopefully.

"Lor, boy, I couldn't tell 'ee. 'Twas before my father's day. But I've a-heard tell as how he was a proper wrong 'un, old Jasper." Dooley finished ramming the tobacco into his pipe and put it back in his pocket again. "And now look—here's young Fauntleroy, coming to call you in to your dinner, I shouldn't wonder."

Sure enough, Fauntleroy was approaching across the yard with a firm and purposeful tread. Moreover, there was something in Fauntleroy's eye that could not be ignored. Obediently the children picked up the musical box and the hatchet and their box of firewood and followed him without further ado.

"Be seein' you!" called out Dooley in farewell as they went, and the children waved back cheerily. They liked Dooley.

When they reached the house the kitchen table was laid for the midday meal (not in the anteroom this time) and Aunt Amethyst was busy dishing up a large and delicious-smelling pie, while Chunky lay curled up on the hearthrug, his nose between his paws, just as if nothing had ever happened.

"What's that you've raked up?" inquired Aunt Amethyst as they entered. She was looking at the music box.

Kit enthusiastically put her treasure on the dresser and set it tinkling out its pretty gay tune.

"We found it up in the loft," explained Richard.

"In the loft?" Aunt Amethyst looked doubtful. "Ah, yes, all that rubbish will have to be cleaned out some day. No one has ventured up there for years. That stairway is too narrow for my liking, and the servants . . . Well, the servants always had some story about the place

being haunted. Goodness knows where these old wives'
tales come from. Anyway, they always avoided it."

The children exchanged glances but said nothing.
Once again some instinctive feeling of secrecy kept them
silent.

"Still," said Kit, "*this* isn't rubbish. May we keep it,
please?"

"Why, of course you may, if it really works. But close
it now, child, and come to the table or your pie will
be cold."

Chapter 7

LADY LAETITIA

"Let's go to the library and tell Michael about this morning," suggested Richard when they had helped with the dishes.

"Oh, yes, let's! I'm looking forward to seeing Michael again," said Kit.

(There wasn't to be a piano lesson this afternoon, for Aunt Amethyst had to take the chair at some sort of meeting in the village and would not be back till teatime.)

"If we can get hold of him . . ." reminded Caroline, as they made their way through the hall.

The library was bright with afternoon sunshine and the sharp brilliance of the winter's day seemed to set everything glinting, both indoors and out. The snowstorm wore its lit-up-from-within look, and almost before Richard had taken it and shaken it up Michael was there beside them.

"I *am* glad to see you," he said at once, "for I've something to tell you. My grandfather says that somewhere about the house is a valuable collection of antique coins. If only we could find them they might prove to be exactly the sort of thing you have in mind. Your aunt might not so much mind selling old *coins.*"

"No," agreed the children.

"Somewhere around the house—he doesn't know where?" queried Richard.

"So I understand," nodded Michael. "It seems they have only recently been missed, but Grandfather feels sure they must still be in the house somewhere. It *may* be that the Scamp made off with them, of course, but Grandfather thinks he has definitely heard of them having been seen since that date."

"The Scamp?"

"You haven't heard of him? It was he who sold the bulk of the estates, and he sold, too, everything else he *could* get rid of. The gaps in the family portraits are due to him—he sold all the really valuable ones. He sold silver that had been in the family since the reign of Henry VII—he would have sold the house, too, if he could. He died unmarried—he was killed hunting—and another branch of the family came into possession: *our* branch. My grandfather's grandfather told him about the coins—it appears they constitute an extremely valuable collection. . . ."

"Well, if they're hidden away somewhere we must set

to work and try to find them," decided Richard instantly. "If they were valuable in your time, Michael, what must they be worth *now!*"

"Yes." Michael flinched a bit. He did not like to be reminded of the gap in time that divided them. "That was what *I* was thinking. Shall we start searching immediately?"

"We could," agreed Caroline. "Aunt Amethyst is out."

"We were going to tell him about this morning," reflected Kit, "but this is more important. The other can wait."

Michael was looking flushed and excited. "It will be a real treasure hunt! And who knows what we may discover, even if we do not find the coins! I have always had a half-formed notion that something might well be hidden in that old sedan chair in the hall, so shall we start with that?"

The children could not remember a sedan chair in the hall, but Michael insisted there was one, and there it was when they went to investigate—standing in the corner by the stairs. It was a high, squarish structure of wood, painted black, and picked out with gold, with side windows at which hung rose-colored curtains of rich brocade. On each outer side were gilded lanterns and, lower down, heavy leather straps through which had once passed the poles that had lifted the chair onto the shoulders of its porters. The little door closed after them, they found, and the seat inside was deeply cushioned, cozy as a featherbed.

"I should think it might lift up, this seat," said Richard thoughtfully, "but somehow . . . I don't know how it is

. . . there seems to be something in the way. . . ."

"Please to leave the seat *alone,* little boy," rebuked a silvery voice, and they all jumped guiltily.

Heavens! How was it they had not seen her? She sat there, as pretty as a picture in her dress of rose brocade, with her powdered hair piled high, a black patch on her cheek, and a narrow black velvet ribbon around her throat. It was her wonderfully tiered skirts that had been getting in Richard's way, and Richard himself was struck speechless.

"I beg your pardon, ma'am," Michael (also pretty well bowled over) answered for him. "We were not aware that the chair was occupied. I do not think I have had the pleasure of meeting you before."

The lady laughed her pretty silvery laugh and flirted her fan a bit. "It appears that one may meet *anyone* in this strange house. No, I do not remember you, child. Are you a Faraday?"

"Yes. I am Michael."

"And I am Lady Laetitia. You were searching for something lost?"

"Well, yes. . . . Have you ever come upon a collection of coins, Lady Laetitia?"

"Fie! I would that I had, boy! I should know well what use to make of them!"

"I don't think she quite understands the sort of coins you mean," whispered Kit to Michael.

Lady Laetitia, who, it seemed, had sharp ears, bridled haughtily. "You mean to infer that I am a simpleton—a half-wit? Place a guard upon your tongue, little girl. The tongue is an unruly member that can work ruin.

Brave men have been hung for less."

Kit maintained a rather disdainful silence.

"I do wish we could get at that seat," muttered Richard, who had retreated well into the background. "I'm sure I'm right, and that it *does* lift up."

"Let's tip her off," returned Kit darkly. "After all, we know jolly well that she's not real."

"Oh, that wouldn't do," reproached Caroline quickly. "That would be violation. Awful things might happen."

"Let 'em," sniffed Kit, who seemed to have taken a dislike to the patched and powdered beauty. "I wouldn't be surprised if she were every bit as bad as the Scamp. If she saw the coins she'd probably make off with them."

Lady Laetitia reached forward and gave Kit's knuckles a sharp rap with her fan. "Take *that,* child—and *that!* How *dare* you, you impudent brat!"

There was a sudden tinkling sound as the fan fell out of Lady Laetitia's trembling fingers and all at once the sedan chair and its occupant had vanished. Alas, so too had Michael.

The three children were left looking at each other in dismay.

"It's all your fault, Kit," said Richard huffily. "Why couldn't you have been more tactful? We may never see her again."

"And who wants to?" demanded Kit dangerously. "What good could she have been to us, anyway? She wouldn't have told us anything about the coins, even if she had known. What's all the fuss about?"

"You're an awful nuisance, that's what," growled Richard. "And now we've lost Michael, too."

Caroline looked rather sadly from one to the other.

"Somehow," she said slowly, "we don't seem to be getting anywhere, do we? It's all very well, finding the snowstorm and knowing Michael, but he lived such a long time ago and the coins have probably been found and sold since then. That's the sort of thing Aunt Amethyst meant when she said everything of value had gone. . . . Oh, I know it's exciting, meeting Michael, and great fun never knowing what's going to happen next, only . . . Well, as far as helping Aunt Amethyst is concerned we're just wasting our time. It's like chasing shadows."

"Yes, shadows," agreed Kit (whose knuckles were still tingling, however). "We want to think of something practical."

It was cold in the hall and, not feeling like another visit to the library, the children made their way back rather disconsolately to the anteroom, where a bright fire was leaping up the chimney and a kettle on a shelf above was singing happily to itself.

"I wonder if Aunt Amethyst has ever thought of taking in paying guests?" pondered Kit, as they gathered around the warm blaze.

"D'you think they'd come?" asked Richard, who was his usual good-humored self again. "I don't!"

"Well, the beds are pretty comfortable," replied Kit, stoutly defending her idea. "And the views are wonderful."

"Both outside and in!" agreed Richard, chuckling. "If the paying guests were to see all that *we* see, then the fame of Farthingales would spread like wildfire. Aunt

Am would be able to charge twice as much as other places!"

"But it's not everyone who'd *care* to see the sort of things we see," pointed out Caroline reasonably. "It would probably work the other way around and frighten them away. People aren't all level-headed like us. They might even be quite scared. Folks usually are, in the presence of psychical phenomena."

"So that's the name you give me, is it?" hissed a silvery voice in their ears.

Richard said afterwards that it was only the kettle beginning to boil, but this was when the shock had worn off and reason had begun to reassert itself once more. Certainly it had sounded remarkably *like* Lady Laetitia, though they couldn't see her anywhere.

"Somehow I don't think paying guests are the answer," said Caroline, looking around her uneasily.

And neither of the other two could find it in their hearts to contradict her.

It was really rather a relief when the cheerful spluttering of the station wagon sounded in the avenue and they heard Fauntleroy bounding to the front door to let his mistress in.

Chapter 8

THE NOT-SO-STATELY HOME

"You know, Aunt Amethyst, you could get quite a bit of money, just showing people *over* Farthingales," said Caroline dreamily that evening.

They were all sitting around the fire in the anteroom. They had just finished their tea, and the smell of hot buttered toast still hung on the air, mingling deliciously with the smell of wood smoke. It had been a lovely tea— toast and scones, home-made butter, oatmeal cookies, apple jelly, and gingerbread—and each one of them now felt thoroughly happy and full and was stretching out his toes to the warmth of the fire in an absolutely abandoned fashion.

"Showing people over Farthingales?" repeated Aunt Amethyst, puzzled.

"Yes. You know—you charge people half a crown.*
After all, it *is* one of the Stately Homes, isn't it?"

Pride of heritage and love of home struggled fiercely
in Aunt Amethyst's mind with honesty and reason, and
the conflict showed visibly in her face. "Well," she said at
last, "I'm afraid it's more one of the Not-So-Stately, but
the compliment is deeply appreciated, child, nonetheless."

"Of course, it would need a lot of cleaning up," observed Richard.

"Of course," agreed Aunt Amethyst with a sidelong
glance at the lordly male.

"But there are three of us," added Richard kindly,
"and we are all young, able-bodied persons. We could
get quite a lot done in a few days."

"And perhaps you could even have the drawing-room
chimney repaired, then we could have a fire in there,"
reflected Caroline. "It would be a worthwhile invest-
ment. It's wonderful how different—how absolutely
smashing—it looks with a fire alight."

Aunt Amethyst looked at her niece with an inscrutable
expression and no doubt she was wondering how Caroline
knew what the room looked like with a fire on the
hearth, but she made no comment except to point out
that neither Stately Homes nor Not-So-Stately ones re-
ceived visitors in the winter.

"That's true enough," agreed Kit quickly (and she
looked rather anxious, hoping that Aunt Amethyst
would not think that the remark had been a hint and
that she, Kit, had told Caroline how cold her hands had

* See page 181 for conversion rates to American dollars.

been during her music lesson). "So really the chimney could wait."

"Could and *must,*" nodded Aunt Amethyst. "Repairs cost money and worthwhile investments must also be necessary ones. The roof leaks, for example, and there are quite a number of broken windowpanes. Visitors would soon leave off coming if word went around that they're likely to find they have stiff necks the day after."

"Then you do think it's a good idea?" urged Caroline eagerly.

"First rate," admitted Aunt Amethyst blandly. "But it wouldn't work."

"Why not?" demanded Richard.

"Well, for one thing, what is there to see? Absolutely nothing. And who, may I ask, is going to show it to them? If you think I've got time to waste . . ."

"But *we* would, of course," broke in Caroline indignantly. "Who else? We'd give all our time to it."

"You wouldn't," contradicted Aunt Amethyst, shaking her head. "You'll be going to school. And then, later on, you'll be going back home again."

School? They all looked at each other aghast. What a perfectly impossible thought! They had forgotten that such things existed even. And the prospect of going back to the house in Hampstead was pretty grim, too—"After all this," as Richard said moodily.

"I suppose you mean that coed school Mother told us about," he added resentfully. "When does it open?"

"January the twenty-third," replied Aunt Amethyst briskly. "Not long now. And your father has paid your fees in advance, so there's no getting out of it."

"Blimey," said Richard, miserably.

"My dear boy, how many more times have I to tell you that I do not admire that vulgar expression? Farthingales may be one of the Not-So-Stately but it has a certain impeccable standard of manners and diction."

"Rats!" ejaculated Richard feebly. "What an oration, Aunt Amethyst!"

"Orations are made to be noted and respected—and I do not care for your second expression any more than the first, Richard."

"Bl . . . cr . . . cripes!" exclaimed Richard.

Aunt Amethyst gave up.

"Let's play checkers," she said, instead.

So they got out the checkerboard and soon the room was full of laughter and excited voices and the trip-trip-tripping of the gaily colored pieces as they were maneuvered across their checkered battleground.

How warm and cosy it all was, thought Caroline, looking around her with deep contentment. Fauntleroy, who was stretched out full length on the hearthrug, dreaming of rabbits, uttered little whines of delight and moans of despair in his sleep; Chunky, who had retired under the table with an old bone, alternately growled and snorted pleasurably. Even the loud and cheerful ticking of the clock on the mantel seemed to be quite human. And then the homely crackle of the oak logs on the hearth suddenly joined in, too—for a wood fire is a companionable creature and never likes to be left out of anything.

"Magic," thought Caroline dreamily. "Absolute magic . . ."

Aunt Amethyst had changed the subject of the Stately Homes. Nevertheless, the children had not put the matter out of their minds and a few days later—on the next wet day, to be more exact—they returned to it again, for one and all felt that it was about the best idea they'd had yet.

"When we were in the village yesterday," said Richard, "I was thinking how nice it would be to see notices up in the shop windows—

FARTHINGALES MANOR

Open Today 2–7 P.M.

2/6 Admission

"It might well," added Richard seriously, "bring in the millennium."

"M'mmm," agreed Caroline. "It certainly seemed to be a very friendly village. I'm sure they'd do all they could to encourage people to come."

"There could be one in the post office, too," nodded Kit, reminiscently. "The postmistress asked after Aunt Amethyst almost as if she were one of the family. . . . I'm glad we went."

They had gone because Caroline had suddenly remembered with something like horror that they had never posted Mrs. Tressider's postcard telling her that they'd arrived.

"Heavens, we'll have her coming down to see what's wrong!" Kit had exclaimed in alarm when the postcard, decidedly dog-eared and crumpled, had been retrieved at length from one of Richard's pockets. "We'd better get it into the mail straight away!"

Aunt Amethyst had said she wouldn't be driving into civilization again for several days (the previous afternoon she had taken them in the car with her to do some shopping in the nearest town, pointing out to them *en route* the unfortunate coed school) so, as it was bright and sunny, they had walked the whole ten miles, to the village and back, in one morning.

"It won't hurt you," Aunt Amethyst had said. "You've got to learn country ways if you want to feel you belong here, and it will give you a splendid appetite for lunch."

It certainly had. It had also given them a pair of aching legs apiece. But they had enjoyed it.

"It was pretty rough going in parts, especially uphill," Richard had admitted in between mouthfuls of delicious curry, "and the wind was against us coming back, too. But it made us feel real country. Also we've got the lay of the land. . . ."

"The hills are pretty tough," Kit said, "but really the roads aren't too bad, and although we're off the beaten track Farthingales does show up from quite a long way off and it looks awfully romantic—anyone with imagination would want to see more of it, I'm sure."

"Yes. Well, I think we ought to follow up our idea of getting the place clean and tidy in readiness for visitors," said Caroline. "After all, we have nearly two weeks before we start school, and if the weather is going to be like this . . ."

They all looked dejectedly out of the window at the pouring rain and the wind whipping the elms and rippling across the puddles in the drive.

". . . We've got to find something to do indoors," finished up Richard for her. "Yes. Supposing we start right now, then?"

"We'll start with the drawing room," nodded Kit enthusiastically. "Of course, we ought really to sweep the chimney first, but as Aunt Amethyst seems to think it should be left alone we'll have to consider it taboo. That means ceilings to start with, then. Well, we'll need long brooms for that, and we'll have to have our heads tied up or we'll be filthy in five minutes. I wonder if there are any overalls handy?"

"We'll first have to ask Aunt Amethyst if she minds," pointed out Caroline. "We'd better find her now, before they go."

For Aunt Amethyst was about to start out for a sale of farm implements at an outlying farm on the moors, taking Dooley with her.

"Modern children!" she exclaimed when she had heard them out. "If they aren't just the world's seventh wonder! Well, go ahead, then, and do what you like, if it will make you happy. Only don't knock the old place down, will you, for I won't get another."

The field was clear!

"Whoopee!" whistled Richard. "We'll get the whole house straight in no time and I bet you anything you like that those antique coins come to light while we're on the job!"

At the end of a couple of hours there had already been quite a transformation worked in the drawing room. The floor had been brushed briskly from end to end, the dust had been shaken out of the curtains, and the sofas and chairs spanked hard, as they had seen their mother do at home.

Mrs. Winthrop, certainly, might have had a critical word or two to say as regards the method of procedure, but, as Kit pointed out, however it was done it was done *properly,* and it did them credit.

The ceiling was now, surely, shades whiter; the chandeliers sparkled and the windows fairly shone, even though Richard, who was tallest, had not been able to reach quite to the top of them from the summit of the ladder.

"You know, I don't agree with Aunt Amethyst," said Caroline, stepping back to the wall to admire their work. "There's lots to see at Farthingales, even in just this room alone. The harp, and the piano in the window, the Chinese cabinet, the old-fashioned armchairs and sofas, the pretty sea-blue color, the chandeliers. . . . Why, I think *any*one would enjoy coming to see this drawing room."

"So do I," agreed Kit. "And I believe she thinks so too, really—only she won't admit it."

"How difficult it is to get some folks to see reason," sighed Caroline. "And when it's all for their own good, too. I'd love showing people around. Even if we *have* got to go to school later on there will still be weekends."

"And Rick said he'd like to come here and help for the holidays, too," nodded Kit. "Why—where *is* Rick, by the way?"

Caroline came out of a reverie with a start. "I think he may have gone to get some more hot water—I saw him go out just a few minutes ago."

And just then the door was flung open dramatically, and *there* was Rick—walking proudly in with Michael!

"It didn't take me any time at all to get him," beamed Richard. "He came at once."

"I was waiting, really," explained Michael.

He looked rather wonderingly at the children, who actually hadn't any idea how comical they looked in the old overalls Mrs. Tidy had found for them, and with their heads tied up with spotted handkerchiefs. Then he transferred his attention to the room. "Everything seems to be very much the same," he observed, pleased.

Now, of course, they had been in the drawing room with Michael before, but on that other occasion it was they who had been in Michael's drawing room and now it was Michael who was in theirs. In that other, earlier, room everything had been much newer, much brighter in color, but essentially the two were the same. Except for the different kind of piano and, Michael insisted, for a portrait hanging on the wall between two windows.

"That's Sir William. He used to be in the portrait gallery. I wonder what has brought him down here?"

"It may be because there *isn't* any picture gallery now. Or perhaps because he seems to match the room," suggested Kit.

"He does, doesn't he," agreed Caroline. "I hadn't noticed before."

Sir William was a young man in his twenties. He had a fine-featured, rather dreamy face, and long flowing curls. He wore an exquisite lace cravat, and there was more lace about his wrists. His stamped velvet coat was indeed exactly the same blue-green tint as the curtains beside him and the chairs below him. The ribbon around his neck was the same cherry-scarlet shade as the Chinese cabinet which brought such a warm note of color into the white-paneled room, and altogether, indeed, Sir William did complete the drawing room as if he had been painted for that very purpose. Moreover, his was the only portrait in the room, the rest being landscapes and flower pieces.

"He's like you, Michael," observed Kit earnestly. "Why, but for the curls you'd be his very double."

"I know," said Michael. "I was always said to be like him, even though we are not the same branch of the family. That's why I noticed him here. Let's go up to the gallery and see the others."

So they went upstairs with Michael, for, after all— who knew?—there *might* be some such room if they only knew where to look for it.

"It used to be *here*," said Michael, puzzled. "You turned left in the corridor at the head of the stairs and it was through this doorway, only there *was* no door. . . ."

"But that's our bedroom," protested Caroline, turning the handle and showing him.

"And mine is here, beyond," added Richard, doing the same.

"Up here it all seems to be quite different," admitted Michael sadly. "The picture gallery used to be my favorite place. The Long Gallery, it was called."

"How I'd love to see it!" exclaimed Kit impulsively.

The despondent look on Michael's face suddenly lifted. "Well, I wonder . . . if *I* tried . . ."

He turned the handle of the girls' room again and—
"Glory be!" gasped Caroline—a blaze of color seemed to
leap out at them: they were in the picture gallery!

"How did you do it?" demanded Richard.

"I do not know at all! But let us make the most of it
while we can," answered Michael with shining eyes.
"See, here is Sir William."

Sure enough, there was the gentleman in the blue coat
with the cravat and the cherry-scarlet ribbon, looking
just as handsome and noble and as like Michael as he
had done downstairs.

"And by golly!" exclaimed Richard, moving on to the
next picture, "look at this dame! If she's not Lady
Laetitia, I'll eat my cap."

Lady Laetitia's black eyes seemed to fairly sparkle out
of the canvas at them.

"You like me?" inquired a familiar voice. "Sir Joshua
has not long finished me—in fact I have only today been
hung."

No one had heard her come into the gallery, but there
she was, indubitably, standing beside them admiring her
own portrait!

"Ah, la, la! Do I not look pretty? But oh, alas! It took
such an *age* to paint me. I wearied so of the long, long
sittings! My lord had boxes of all the new plays sent
down from London that I might while the time away
reading. But Sir Joshua did not care for that idea. And
then, perchance, my lord might even take a fancy to the
play himself. I might be in the very middle of a delicious
wicked comedy of Mr. Wycherley's and my lord would
steal it from me. . . . But la, the result is supremely

worth it all, do you not think so?"

"I do indeed, ma'am!" agreed Michael. He was pink with pleasure and he spoke rather bashfully—and, really, Kit for one could have slapped him, he looked so . . . so *besotted*. (This was Kit's own word and she felt that it fitted exactly.)

Lady Laetitia's attention now became focused full upon Michael.

"Ah, the same little boy! Have you discovered your coins yet, child?"

At this Kit reached boiling point. "They aren't Michael's, Lady Laetitia, and he's not a little boy or a child, either. The coins have no intrinsic value and only numismatics would be interested in them. They have great value as collectors' pieces and that is all."

Kit was specially using big words in order to confound Lady Laetitia, and she had got one of them wrong which is always the risk when you use anything you're not accustomed to. But, as Lady Laetitia was really rather a featherbrain, she was unlikely to have noticed.

"You are a numismatist?" inquired Lady Laetitia sweetly of Kit.

"No, she isn't," Richard answered bluntly for her. "We'd just like to find the coins so's Aunt Amethyst can sell 'em."

"If she wants to, that is, of course," added Caroline quickly.

Lady Laetitia smiled kindly. "Old coins . . . ? And they have a value?"

"Why, yes!" Richard assured her eagerly. "I've been keeping my eye on the paper since we heard about the collection, and at Christie's a Charles II coin of 1668 was sold for £165 the other day, and a five-guinea piece of the reign of James II for £140. It dated from 1687. Best of all, there was a Henry IV Calais noble, and that brought £780!"

"But, of course, you *wouldn't* know about them, would you," Kit conceded generously, "because most of them *weren't* antique in *your* day."

There was a guffaw of laughter from somewhere behind and, turning around, the children saw that a gentleman—was it Sir William?—had joined them. If he *was* Sir William he was older than in his portrait, however, and wore a black wig instead of his own long curls.

"You perceive how it is, Laetitia, my love?" chuckled this worthy. "We are ourselves antique!"

The children looked a little uncomfortable. Except Kit.

"We didn't mean to be rude," apologized Richard politely.

Kit would dearly have liked to contradict him, but she thought better of it at the last moment. "Oh, Sir William, you *are* like Michael!" she exclaimed instead, gazing at him ardently. "I'd have known you *any*where!"

Another roar of laughter came from the amused Sir William, but Lady Laetitia did not seem so happy.

"Come, my love," said she, putting a guiding hand firmly on her lord's arm. "Let us not be diverted from the matter at hand. There are woodcocks for supper, and after that we will play backgammon."

They walked away down the gallery together and Kit

watched them go with satisfaction.

"Woodcocks for *supper?*" echoed Richard. "And it *is* getting dark outside. Gosh, how long have we been up here?"

"I wouldn't worry," advised Michael. "It will be daylight again when we go downstairs—you'll see. But wait one moment. I wish to correct you. That was not Sir William. *He* lived in the time of Charles II—his portrait is dated 1669. That gentleman was Sir Rodney—he has the same Faraday features, but he belongs to a later day. He is Lady Laetitia's husband. I have found out quite a lot about them since I last saw you. This portrait of Lady Laetitia was painted by Sir Joshua Reynolds in 1770, you notice, so you see they were living in the reign of George III."

"Jumping snakes, you sound like a family tree, old boy," grinned Richard. "Not to mention 1066 and all that. You sure know your history."

"Ah, Mr. Allardyce sees to that," smiled Michael. "But tell me, now, was that true, about the value of certain coins?"

"Absolutely," Richard assured him. "You can read it if you like. I cut it out."

"Then," said Michael impressively, "if what my grandfather tells me is correct, the Faraday Collection must be worth a small fortune."

"We thought it might." Richard nodded.

The children looked at each other longingly, and they all stood silent for a moment, thinking about it.

Outside, the winter twilight was deepening, and shadows were creeping into the Long Gallery, subduing the glowing colors of the pictures. A little wind was whispering around the windows and somewhere, far away, they heard a dog, barking and barking.

"If *only* we could find them," groaned Caroline. "We *must* find them."

"Have you told your Aunt Amethyst yet?" inquired Michael.

"No, we haven't told her anything yet—not even about you. Somehow or other we don't think she would believe us." Caroline smiled rather wryly. "She'd tell us we were seeing things. And so we are, I suppose, in a way."

Michael smiled sadly. "And so am I, I suppose—in a way. It's strange, isn't it—you in your day and I in mine. Perhaps, some time, we may meet as equals. . . ."

"Yes," said Kit wistfully.

And Richard flung his arm comfortingly around the other boy's shoulders. "We *are* equals, really—we're equals *now.*"

But Michael, wiser, only shook his head.

Outside, the little wind still whispered about the casements. The dog was still barking. . . .

And the barking grew nearer and nearer and louder and louder, until at last it seemed to be just outside the door. Then came a scratching noise as well, and a low whine—and suddenly they realized that it was Fauntleroy; that they were standing in Richard's bedroom and that Michael, Lady Laetitia, Sir Rodney, and the picture gallery—not to mention the gathering dusk outside the windows—had all vanished like moonshine.

Chapter 9

WAYS AND MEANS

Fauntleroy and Chunky, it seemed (for they were both there, outside the door), had come to call them down to the midday meal. Aunt Amethyst had returned from the sale and Mrs. Tidy was dishing up rabbit casserole just as they entered the kitchen.

"I have seen the drawing room." Aunt Amethyst beamed. "It looks fit for a princess!"

"Oh, but it's not nearly finished," protested Kit "We've got to wash down the white paneling yet, and dust and polish."

"That thou hasn't then," chided a cracked old voice. "I've dusted and polisht it meself, I hev, whilst ye've been gaddin' about above stairs. The idea of it, runnin' off an' leavin' a job half finisht! Thou'rt like all these

present-day children—can't stop at one thing for five
minnits. Grasshoppers, that's what ye be."

The children looked uneasily at Mrs. Tidy, wondering
how much she knew, and then at each other, sorely dis-
comfited. They didn't want to have to explain about
Michael, but the criticism was very galling.

"Well, never mind who did it." Aunt Amethyst smiled
reassuringly. "The important thing is it's done, more or
less, and it looks *wonderful!*" This was praise indeed.

"Now wash your hands and come and enjoy your
meal," she added. "A laborer is worthy of his hire."

For the next few days the children were full of enthusiasm for their self-imposed task, with little or nothing
to hinder them at it. Sometimes the weather was fine and
sunny, and then they went exploring the grounds or
following the river out onto the moor. But, for the most
part, it was bleak and gray with little to tempt them
out of doors. Inside the house Aunt Amethyst seemed
happy enough to leave them to their own devices, and for
some reason or other Michael failed to materialize,
however hard they sought him. So the great Cleaning
Drive, as Richard called it, went on rapidly.

Soap and water and elbow grease were applied un-
stintingly to every neglected part of the house. Windows
took on a sparkle, oak floors shone, paneling gleamed
like silk where it had been polished or washed down.
Kit said she had never chased so many cobwebs in her
life. "I'm beginning to feel like an old witch," she said,
leaning exhausted on her broom.

Nor was cleaning their only activity. Now and then

they would take time off to tap the walls for hollow spaces or secret passages, always with the thought of those antique coins in mind—the forgotten Faraday Collection. But nothing came to light. The old house hid its secrets jealously.

Sometimes they came upon rooms they had not noticed before, big bare rooms filled with dust-sheeted furniture that they couldn't do much about, and sometimes they would look up from their labors and see Mrs. Tidy standing in the doorway watching them, wizened and bent, an inscrutable expression on her face. She never spoke a word, and if the children looked as if they might be going to say something to her she simply vanished, noiselessly, like a little old wicked fairy.

Yet they knew, of course, that there was nothing like that, really, about Mrs. Tidy. "It's just that she feels she has to keep her eye on us and make sure that we don't break anything," as Kit said, amused.

Then one morning Richard had a bright idea.

"Let's make an inventory of all the furniture and pictures and things. We can enter the value of everything in a column at the side, so that Aunt Am knows just where she stands and what she's worth."

"But would *we* know what the things are worth?" asked Caroline doubtfully.

"We could get some idea by watching the paper. Every day there are reports of sales at Christie's and Sotheby's. I'm going to start a notebook right away."

Richard was always starting notebooks; his locker at home was crammed full of them, mostly unfinished. Still, this was a good idea. "As we finish cleaning each room we can make an inventory of what's in it and add everything up to a total," agreed Kit.

So the next fine day they walked across the moors to the village again and Richard bought his notebook at the post office.

Even Caroline and Kit had caught the craze now. "A Spode dessert service of twenty-eight pieces realized 340 guineas at Christie's yesterday," read out Kit from the morning paper the following day. "Aunt Amethyst said the one in the anteroom closet is Spode. D'you think it's worth all that?"

"Could be," said Richard optimistically. "Only there aren't twenty-eight pieces. Still, I'll put it down." He made a neat entry in his notebook and wrote "340" in the column at the end, which was headed firmly: "Value in Guineas."

"Then there's that flower picture behind the harp in the drawing room," went on Kit, encouraged. "It's by Huysum. Aunt Amethyst told me, the day I had my first music lesson. Well, a flower piece here catalogued as Huysum fetched 450 guineas."

"Flower piece—Huysum—450," wrote down Richard at once.

At this point Caroline, anxious not to appear backward, picked up the paper and reported that a Stuart needlework carpet had gone for 880 guineas at Sotheby's. Nobody made any comment, however, for each of them, including Caroline, secretly felt that all the carpets at Farthingales were so threadbare that they would not be worth a penny, even if one of them did happen to be Stuart needlework.

"And £520 for a pair of Derby pigeon tureens and covers!" she added excitedly.

Ah, now, that was something like! There were white pigeon tureens in the anteroom cabinet as large as life! Only . . . were they Derby?

"Let's go and ask," suggested Richard.

But Aunt Amethyst (who knew all about the inventories and the notebook, of course) only smiled a rather sad smile on hearing the news, so that there was really no need at all for her to tell them that they weren't.

"It's as I've said before—everything of real value was sold years ago. Other things seemed to just vanish. There was a rumor of historical miniatures, for instance, and certain valuable books, and an ivory-brisé fan, not to mention another one painted by Antoine Watteau that was said to have belonged to a queen. But what happened to them I couldn't say. Maybe someone will come upon them poked away, somewhere, some day. But not in my time. Too late to help *me*. . . . Not that I'm complaining. Why, I wouldn't know how to fill my days if I hadn't to pinch and scrape and contrive. It's a challenge—it brings zest into living. There's a certain happiness in having to struggle. I thrive on it."

"But one day you'll be old," reproved Caroline, "and then you won't be *able* to struggle."

"Nonsense, child. I'm old now. One foot in the grave. Oh, for heaven's sake, don't worry your heads about *me!*"

"Wasn't there even a portrait gallery at Farthingales?" asked Richard cunningly. "Most old houses of this sort have one."

"Once there was," nodded Aunt Amethyst. "But more

accommodation was needed some time in the last century and so the Long Gallery was converted into three bedrooms. Yours is one, Richard, and the girls' is another. You wouldn't know—the work was done so well and the newer paneling matches the old exactly. All the portraits of any value, including a Reynolds and a Romney, were sold about that time, too, to meet death duties. Only one remains—Sir William Faraday, who now hangs in the drawing room."

"Yes. . . ." The children tried hard not to look too knowing. "Who was Sir William?"

"He lived here in the days of Charles II. Come into the drawing room and let us have a good look at him. . . . He's handsome, isn't he? The portrait was painted in 1669. A typical Faraday face, although he was another branch of the family. Your grandfather was very like him. . . . Richard too may be a little—just a little—like him, one day."

Richard's sisters started visibly and turned around to look more closely at their brother, who appeared acutely uncomfortable. "Wasn't there a Sir Rodney?" he asked, to change the subject. "There's a tablet in the village church to Sir Rodney Faraday. We saw it yesterday."

"Ah, yes, Rodney lived in George III's day. He had a son who was a great trial to him, known later as the Scamp. The boy took after his flighty mother, I fear." Kit shot an I-told-you-so look at Caroline and Richard. "But theirs was yet another branch of the family. The Scamp died unmarried and the place came to our people."

So it was all true—all that Michael had said. Not that

they had ever doubted him . . . But to hear it all again from Aunt Amethyst gave them a queer feeling they could not quite explain.

"Carry on with your inventories, by all means, if it amuses you," concluded Aunt Amethyst, as they closed the drawing-room door, "but it's as I've told you—practically everything went long ago. There's only one *really* valuable object in the house now, and that is . . ."

"Yes?"

"Well, it's only small . . . It is an old-fashioned paper-weight, very rare—a snowstorm—on the library mantel-piece. . . . You've probably never noticed it."

"Probably not," said Kit in a strangled voice, glancing desperately at the others.

"But mind you," added Aunt Amethyst severely, look-ing them straight in the eye, "I wouldn't part with it. Not for all the tea in China."

They all let out their breath in relief.

"So she knows the snowstorm is something rather spe-cial," reflected Richard later on. "I wonder . . ."

"Perhaps when *she* was young . . ." Kit nodded.

"Perhaps you *have* to be young to see the magic." Caroline screwed up her forehead with the effort of thinking it out. "It may be she's forgotten now—if she did ever know—just what extraordinary powers it has. But she remembers enough to know she could never sell it, however valuable it may be."

"Could be," agreed Richard. "Well, thank goodness for that."

Chapter 10

MR. ALLARDYCE

That was the night when Caroline couldn't sleep. She lay awake, turning first this way and then that, enviously aware of Kit's regular breathing in the other half of the bed, staring at the Hundred Eyes and trying in vain to count them in a desperate effort to win oblivion. But all that happened was that she became more awake than ever.

Each tiny sound became intensified. She could hear the scamper of mice in the empty rooms overhead, the faint whisper of the wind in the ivy and creepers around the window, the far-off music of the river, as, swollen by the recent rains, it went racing and leaping over its scattered boulders. And then there came, too, a sound unlike these others—a sound more definite, heavier, nearer: the sound of footsteps in the quiet room.

Caroline stiffened. How dark the room was! The Hundred Eyes did so little to lighten it, for all the comfort it gave. The footsteps came nearer, till they were in the room, here beside her bed—she was almost sure of it. . . . And then a shadow passed over the Hundred Eyes, blotting them out completely for a few seconds—and she *knew*.

Caroline experienced a moment's intense fear, and her first instinct was to bury her head deep under the bed-clothes; then something stronger than panic seemed to take command. She wanted to know who it was. . . .

Shivering with cold or fear or excitement (she really didn't know which), Caroline slipped out of bed and reached for her warm bathrobe, and it was then, as she knotted the cord about her waist and stood hesitant, that she suddenly realized that she was not in her bed-room: this was the Long Gallery! The paneled walls, the portraits, the long expanse of shining floor, were all clearly visible now in the subdued light of the moon as it looked in at the tall windows. And just ahead of her moved a dark figure—whether a man's or a woman's she could not tell—heavily cloaked and hooded.

Caroline knew that she was going to follow it; indeed, that she *must* follow it. As she stole down the long room, it somehow appeared to grow lighter, even though the moon went behind a cloud. She was suddenly aware of the pictured faces on the walls looking down on her—it seemed in wonder. And well they might, she thought—she, Caroline, who so hated the dark!

And then she realized that although she hated it, she

had never really been *afraid* of it. It was only the sense of being stifled. And that vanished once one took action. "You must learn to look *through* the dark and not *at* it," a voice seemed to say in her ear.

And so she stole on after the dark figure with a feeling of mounting triumph and excitement.

She expected to hear the door click as the intruder passed through, but she didn't. All was silence. Then she realized that there was, of course, no door there, anyway, as Michael had said. . . . The dark figure was gliding on in front of her through a carved archway where the door would have been. Now they were on the stairs—and the treads creaked eerily! Would anyone else hear? she wondered anxiously. But apparently no one did and they reached the hall and passed, silent as wraiths, into the drawing room.

Just inside the door she stood motionless and, hidden by a tall screen, watched the slow progress of her quarry around the room. The moonlight shone full in through the great tall windows, lying in broad shafts and pools like silver water across the floor, glinting on the strings of the harp, drawing mysterious responses from the long mirrors. The whole room seemed lit up with the gentle light and, as the cloaked figure reached the window nearest her, Caroline saw clearly the illumined face: it was Mr. Allardyce!

He passed, indeed, so near to her on his way back to the hall that she could not have escaped being seen if he had chanced to look her way. But he did not do so, for he seemed to be listening, watching for something and, in fact, he strained forward as if he heard it in front of him.

Caroline herself could discern nothing, but she followed Mr. Allardyce through the little anteroom (empty of furniture, she noticed, and looking just like the inside of a wooden box) and out into the hall again. The sedan chair was there, in its corner by the stairs, and the floor was spread with a sumptuous carpet she had not seen before. The heavy, red leather *portière* over the library door was the same, however, and like one in a dream she followed Mr. Allardyce through.

He was standing at one of the windows, looking out over the moonlit garden. Presently he turned and went around the room, running his hand gently over the books on their ordered shelves. Here and there his hand seemed to detect some irregularity, denoting a gap perhaps where one was missing, and he paused to investigate; he even mounted the miniature stepladder and reached to the top shelves. And all the time Caroline stood there in the shadows, invisible in her dark bathrobe, watching him.

Once there was the sound of footsteps somewhere— she couldn't gauge just where—and Mr. Allardyce heard them, too, and came down from the ladder and stood tense, waiting. But the footsteps passed, and nobody came. Mr. Allardyce returned to his searching for a while, leaving the bookshelves and turning his attention to the escritoire instead; then presently, having found what it was he wanted, perhaps, he went toward the fireplace, opened a door, and vanished.

Left alone, Caroline too went toward the fireplace, but there was no sign of any exit. Then she remembered the stairway in the wall and the section of shelving that had swung back invisibly into place. Yes . . . and she remembered the old cloak, too, hanging in the closet at the top of them. So that was who it had belonged to!

Should she try to follow Mr. Allardyce? wondered Caroline. But the door had closed completely after him, she did not know where or how to find the concealed spring that evidently opened it, and, try as she would, her questing fingers could discover nothing in the half-dark. As she stood there hesitating she heard footsteps again, slow and stealthy and quite close at hand—in the wall? All at once, somewhere afar off, there was a piercing scream, long and shrill and then suddenly silent as if it had been muffled by someone. It made Caroline's heart thump and her pulse race, and she stood there half paralyzed, wondering what was going to happen next.

But nothing did. Silence settled steadily down over the room again and gradually the beating of Caroline's heart slowed down, too, and she began to wonder if she had imagined it all. Only she knew she hadn't. . . .

Dazed and tired and rather frightened, wondering what it was all about, she stumbled back to the hall and, turning the matter over in her mind as she went, found herself upstairs and back in bed again almost before she knew.

"Tomorrow we must tell Michael," was her last conscious thought as she fell asleep.

Kit and Richard could hardly believe the story of Caroline's adventure when they heard it the following morning before going down to breakfast.

"You who always hated the dark!" exclaimed her twin.

"But it didn't *seem* dark, somehow. That was the funny part. I wasn't the tiniest bit afraid. Somehow I just *had* to see what was going on, and nothing else mattered."

"And all the time it was just Mr. Allardyce, the tutor," mused Richard wonderingly. "You know, it seems to me—have you ever thought, kids?—those coins we're looking for: they *may* have been stolen, as Michael said. And it may not have been the Scamp. They had only discovered the loss, the old man told Michael. Well, your story, Caro, makes me wonder whether perhaps the culprit might be Mr. Allardyce."

"It *is* suspicious," agreed Caroline. "Only . . ."

"Only what?"

"Mr. Allardyce doesn't look like a thief."

"They never do."

"Well . . ." Caroline suddenly recollected the intent way the tutor had looked at them when Michael had asked his grandfather about hidden treasure. "You could be right," she admitted grudgingly.

"And if the coins, other things as well, quite likely," added Kit sagely. "Thieves don't stop at one thing. In a house like this all sorts of valuable items could slowly vanish, without anyone being the wiser for ages."

"Small things," agreed Caroline thoughtfully. She remembered the queer behavior of Mr. Allardyce in the library. "Valuable books, perhaps, and those miniatures Aunt Amethyst mentioned, and the fans. . . . Yes, it's an idea. Well, if you're right, Rick, what's the use of searching any more?"

"But don't you see? That's just it!" replied Richard excitedly. "Maybe Mr. Allardyce *was* feathering his nest, and hiding the things away somewhere one by one so that he could take them all away together. And perhaps something happened, and he never did, and that's why we see him . . . that's why he comes back—because he has something on his mind."

"Gosh, what a brain!" teased Kit.

Caroline, however, was impressed. "And so, if we watch Mr. Allardyce, and follow him—you never know —we may find the coins and the other things?"

"Yes. That's why we *see* him," repeated Richard positively.

There was silence for a while as they all surveyed the situation in this new aspect.

"It's fantastic really, isn't it?" Caroline said at last. "It all started with the snowstorm. At first we couldn't even get Michael without shaking it up—now we seem to have the whole family milling around! Grandfather Faraday and Mr. Allardyce, Lady Laetitia, Sir Rodney. . . . It makes you wonder who will turn up next."

Kit nodded. "All things have to have a beginning, I suppose. It seems we somehow set a whole world in motion when we shook the snowstorm."

"I think we see them all because we *believe* in them," mused Caroline, "and that encourages them—gives them something to hold on to . . . to grow by. . . ."

"That's it," agreed Richard. "That's what I've always thought, right from the start. After all, lots of people *wouldn't* believe in them—as we've said before, they might even be scared. And, you know, it's not really so much that we *see* them as that we get back into the past— *their* past. They're not *here*—we're *there*."

"Yes. . . . And it's rather odd, really, that we *don't* ever feel afraid," reflected Kit, "because it's a perfectly extraordinary situation."

"We might—if there were something evil—wicked," said Caroline slowly. "I felt afraid when I saw the old man in the loft—Burbage, if that's who he was. That's why I think . . . that's why I *know* that he was up to no good. Besides, I wasn't back in the past when I saw *him*. But with Mr. Allardyce I was, and I didn't feel afraid either, not at first—only curious."

"Well, let's go along to the library after breakfast and see what Michael makes of it all," suggested Richard. "That is, of course, if we can get hold of him. . . . He may be able to explain it."

Chapter 11

A JUNE AFTERNOON

The children had planned to turn their attention to the library that morning, in any case, so after they had helped with the dishes (Richard breaking a plate and Caroline a milk jug in their haste to be finished) they got into their cleaning togs, as Kit called them, and, gathering together all their usual paraphernalia of buckets, brushes, brooms, mops, dusters, soap, and water, they set off in high hopes.

As they opened the library door the clock on the mantelpiece began to strike ten.

"Good," said Richard. "We've got nearly three hours today. We ought . . ."

And then he broke off, and they each drew back in astonishment, for the library shutters had all been half closed. The light that filtered in was dim, almost spectral, but it was not too dark for them to see the gaunt figure of Michael's grandfather asleep in the leather armchair with a handkerchief spread over his face. The round mahogany table in the middle of the room was strewn with open ledgers and dog-eared accounts, and there was also a bowl of roses on it, filling the air with their delicate scent.

Then they saw Michael standing there, smiling, with a finger on his lips.

"Old Pybus always closes the shutters for Grandfather's afternoon nap. Don't let us wake him . . . the agent will be here soon. . . . Oh, I'm so glad you have come. I knew you would. . . . You have something to tell me?"

"Yes. But how do you know?" asked Richard.

"I don't know. I was just somehow aware of it."

"Well, it's Caroline who had the adventure. Go on, Caro. Start at the beginning."

They all moved over to the window, out of earshot of the old man. Caroline launched into her story and Michael heard it through in silence.

"It is certainly very strange," he said at last. "I always knew there was something about my good Mr. Allardyce . . . something that I could not quite fathom. But . . ." and here Michael hesitated. "But I always considered him perfectly honest," he added firmly.

"Then you don't think he's feathering his nest?" said Richard, disappointed.

"He has no nest to feather. He is devoted to my grandfather, and to my aunt also, and is content to live here with us."

"Yes, but Richard means might he not be hiding things away—hoarding them, against the time when he might be able to use them. . . . Well, *sell* them?"

"I find it uncommonly difficult to believe," said Michael, looking unhappy.

"But why else should he wander around at dead of night? And then that scream—what about that? It was bloodcurdling."

"Well, I think I can explain the scream. It must have been old Barnabas, a barn owl that gets in the garrets sometimes and keeps us awake with his snoring. He does shriek if he's disturbed, and it sounds extraordinarily human."

"It could have been Barnabas, then," conceded Caroline fairly. "But, Michael, Aunt Amethyst was telling us about things that just seemed to have vanished into the blue—valuable miniatures, for instance, and books, and a fan painted by Watteau. . . ."

"I don't know about any fan, but we have miniatures of Lord Darnley and Mary Queen of Scots which are valuable, certainly. They have been locked away in the escritoire because the light was fading the colors, I think. There's a secret drawer—I can show you." Michael went across to the escritoire and at a touch a little drawer sprung out where none had been visible. But there were no miniatures in it. It was quite empty. And Michael stared at it in dismay.

"You see?" said Richard.

"Yes . . ." agreed Michael unwillingly. "Did Mr. Allardyce go to the escritoire last night, Caroline?"

"Yes, I'm afraid he did. But most of the time he seemed

to be concentrating on the bookshelves, as if there were gaps there."

They looked around the room at the orderly rows of books, but the handsome, calf-bound volumes seemed to present a quite unbroken front.

"We could go around examining," suggested Richard.

But Michael was quick to discourage that idea. "Not just now. We should be sure to awaken my grandfather, and he's had such a tiring morning. It has been so hot."

"Hot?"

"Why, yes—June usually is, isn't it?"

"*June?*" The children peeped through the shutters and, sure enough, the garden was drenched in the golden sunshine of a summer afternoon. The scent of roses drifted in, and honeysuckle, and new-mown hay.

"Oh, well . . ." said Richard uneasily, quite at a loss for words.

Caroline was looking thoughtful. "I wonder if it was summer when I went stalking Mr. Allardyce?" she mused. "That might explain why I didn't feel in the least cold. . . ."

"Michael," she said out loud, "I've just remembered something I want to ask you: what does Mr. Burbage look like?"

"Old Gaffer Burbage? He's a rather dirty old man with long white hair."

"And a beaky nose?"

"You could call it beaky—yes."

"Then I *saw* him, Michael! In the old coachhouse!"

"Things are always happening to Caroline," grumbled Richard. "Kit and I didn't notice a thing. It makes me wonder if it really *was* Mr. Allardyce she saw last night."

"But it *was!* I *did* see him," Caroline protested hotly. "Only seeing Burbage was different, Michael. I wasn't back in the past then, as I was last night. And I felt terribly afraid. So I think it's pretty certain he was a cunning old rogue."

"He may well be," nodded Michael. "There's many a tale told of old Burbage. They say he's not quite right in the head. . . . But once, and not so long ago, either, he used to be respectable enough—yes, and respected, too. Mrs. Burbage was housekeeper then, and he was one of our coachmen. That's how it was you saw him in the coachhouse."

Caroline looked disappointed. "We thought he might have been up to mischief. But if he had a right there I suppose there's nothing in it."

Just then they heard the sound of wheels outside.

"It's Mr. Peabody, the agent," said Michael, peering through the shutters at a smart, stout little man driving a gig and briskly trotting horse up the lime avenue. "He'll be coming in here. Let us go in the garden out of the way."

One of the windows stood wide open. He drew the shutters apart noiselessly and they all climbed over the low sill onto the smooth turf outside. The sun was so hot it was like a weight on their backs.

"And we with our winter clothes on, too!" as Kit said with a groan.

"Where shall we go?" asked Michael.

"What about the coachhouse?" suggested Caroline. "Then I can show you where . . ."

"Where you saw old Burbage?" Michael finished for her. "Yes, let us, then. And do keep in the shade, all of you. Those strange garments were certainly not intended for a summer's day."

"You're telling us," agreed Richard ruefully. "And we have more on than we usually wear, too, because we were going to clean the library, and it's jolly cold in there without a fire. It was winter till we met you!"

Michael smiled. "The snowstorm again."

"But it wasn't—we didn't shake it—we didn't have a chance."

"No, but I did. _I_ shook it. I wanted to see you," and Michael laughed at their surprised faces.

"So it works both ways?" said Richard.

"Of course. Well, here is the coachhouse."

The children looked in amazement at the imposing building, hardly recognizing it, so smart it was with its newly painted brickwork, its white painted doors and windows, and neat graveled court in front.

"Why, it seems to be part of the house," said Kit.

"So it is. Farthingales is Tudor, built around a quadrangle."

"But it's not in the least like this _now!_" exclaimed Caroline.

"You mean in your day," corrected Michael.

"All right, then—in our day," Caroline amended hastily. "In our day there is just the house and then, a little way off, the coachhouse and the woodhouse. All this is quite strange to us."

"It might almost be another place," agreed Richard.

They stood looking at it as if it were a picture in a

book. The court in which they stood was surrounded on all sides except the north by stabling and dairies. Looking back the way they had come, they saw that the house itself filled up all this north side, its familiar windows opening onto a wide terrace laid out with lawns and flowerbeds with steps down to the gravel sweep where they now stood. Behind the children a broad archway in the side opposite the house gave admission to the courtyard from the avenue.

"It was built against the great gales that sweep the moor," explained Michael, "and to catch every little bit of sun there is."

"It still does that," agreed Kit.

They looked at it all rather wistfully. There was the same familiar porch where Fauntleroy had welcomed them on the night of their arrival, and the same great south windows where Aunt Amethyst liked to sit sometimes with her sewing or her accounts. The hall door stood open and they saw within the same great cavernous fireplace that was never lit now because it took more fuel than Aunt Amethyst could afford, and because, too, it had bats in the chimney and loose bricks, like the one in the drawing room.

Caroline sighed. "Yes, in our day there is just the house," she repeated. "I suppose the rest of these buildings fell into ruin and had to be pulled down long ago. It's as we've told you before, Michael. Things are different now—in our day, I mean! People can't afford to keep so much up."

"Well, now let us go inside," said Michael.

The inside of the coachhouse proved to be as unrecognizable as the outside, with its shining carriages, traps, and gaily painted gigs, and its wall hung with harness and horse brasses. There was no stone stairway up the wall to an open loft—the loft itself was there, but it was walled up.

"It doesn't *need* a stairway," said Michael when Caroline remarked upon this. "The loft is reached by a corridor from the house that runs along the top of all these outbuildings. You know the green baize door in the servants' wing? That gives access to it."

But the children had to confess that their Farthingales hadn't a servants' wing and that green baize doors were nonexistent.

"Anyway, that explains how all the old furniture got up there," observed Richard. "I've often wondered how they dragged it up those narrow steps."

"It would also explain how old Burbage appeared to come through the wall," said Caroline. "He seemed to walk into the loft from a place that would be just on the other side of the wall."

"And that is just where the door *is*," said Michael.

"So, you see, I *did* see him." Caroline shot a look of triumph at Richard.

A rather surly-looking groom was making a vast to-do about washing down one of the carriages (and quite understandably regarding Master Michael's queer-looking playmates with the utmost suspicion) or they might have had quite an enjoyable time inspecting all the various sorts of vehicles.

As it was, Michael suggested that they might like to explore the gardens instead and, it being so hot, the children decided on the more wooded parts of the grounds where they could count on cool shade.

They passed out of the quadrangle through the stone archway and started off down the avenue.

"What's that curious structure?" asked Richard, pointing to a sort of stone pavilion or summer house standing on a slight eminence some distance away, surrounded by trees.

"Oh, that's the gazebo," replied Michael. "Haven't you seen it? It was built by one of the Papist Faradays in Cromwell's day. They say there is an underground passage running from it to the house. I told you how they used to hold mass up in the attics. Well, it was a very dangerous thing and if a priest were discovered he was likely to be imprisoned and tortured. After the Restoration the passage was said to be used by smugglers; more recently, they say it was put in order and used quite openly by the household in various ways."

"How odd!" exclaimed Kit. "Whereabouts in the house does it come out?"

"I never knew—I have never been able to find any passage."

"There is the secret passage from the attic to the library," reminded Richard.

"Yes, but that wasn't originally secret. Houses of the time Farthingales was built didn't have staircases like ours. They had great halls reaching to the roof and the stairways were just flights of stone steps in the thickness of the wall. Most of them would have been bricked up, but someone must have decided to preserve this one."

"Well, it must have come in very useful for that

priest," remarked Kit, "and perhaps this other passage you speak of links up with it in some way."

They had reached the gazebo now, and were standing within it. "There's probably a trapdoor here somewhere," reflected Michael, looking at the stone-paved floor. "But possibly it only opens from below. I've spent hours—days—searching but I have never found a single clue."

"Does it matter?" queried Caroline. "Look at the view instead: isn't it *heavenly!*"

Michael rested his arms on the stone balustrading and looked out down the winding, tree-filled valley to the moors and the sparkling sea. "Yes. And some day it will all be mine. . . . Mine!"

The children regarded him sympathetically; Caroline, indeed, with frank envy. But they did not say anything, for one and all were thinking of *their* Farthingales, desolate and neglected, with fallen tiles and broken windows and Aunt Amethyst struggling to save it all from further ruin.

"What exactly *is* your time, Michael?" asked Richard at last. "What year is it now?"

"It is 1832."

The children exchanged glances. In one hundred and thirty-six years how rapidly had Farthingales gone down-hill!

"1832?" repeated Richard aloud. "Then William IV has just come to the throne."

"That is so," agreed Michael, absently. "Listen! Do you hear the river?"

"Yes. And see it, too, but the trees hide most of it, don't they. Where is the waterfall? Or perhaps there isn't one at all in your day?"

"There is. And you can just see it—up there behind the house."

"*I* can't see it."

"Look—*there!* You're not looking high enough."

Richard glanced calculatingly at the balustrading. "Perhaps I'll do better if I climb up here." Holding on to one of the columns, he clambered up. "Oh, yes, I see it now. . . . Gosh! What's happening?"

"Goodness!" cried Kit in horror. "Look out, Rick! You're bringing the whole thing down."

Sure enough, the section of balustrading on which Richard was so precariously poised was wobbling dangerously. Then, all at once, the floor seemed to give way beneath the children, too. There was a sudden crash and down, down, down they all went into darkness.

Caroline, Kit, and Richard were dimly aware of Michael's voice, excited even as he fell: *"It's the secret passage!"*

Then there was the lapping sound, and oh, the nasty cold wet *feel* of running water. . . .

The darkness had vanished. So had Michael.

"Silly!" Kit, to her astonishment, found herself saying. "Why can't you look where you're going when you're carrying a bucket of soapsuds?"

Wet and shaken, the three children picked themselves up from the library doorway and could find nothing on the floor to account for Richard having tripped up.

Moreover, the clock on the mantelpiece was still striking ten, solemnly, placidly—just as if nothing at all had happened.

Chapter 12

SNOWED IN

"And perhaps it *hadn't!*" said Caroline later on, when they had finished talking about the strange adventure. "Perhaps nothing *had* happened. Perhaps it was, after all, just a sort of dream."

"We've said so before," agreed Kit. "Every time."

"I'll tell you what," suggested Richard. "This afternoon we'll go and see if the gazebo is still there. And if it is . . ."

"Yes—if it is? What will that prove?"

"Well, we might find the secret passage. At least we know that putting our weight on a certain section of balustrading causes a trapdoor in the floor to open."

"Do we?" countered Kit, skeptically.

"Well, we can try."

Going to the window, Caroline gazed down the drive. "Surely we'd have noticed it before if it were still there? It would be in the Long Grove, of course, but even so, in wintertime it would be visible among the trees."

"It's quite likely in ruins now," reflected Richard, "but the site would still be there, and the trapdoor leading down into the passage."

"All covered up with rubble and fallen masonry," nodded Kit practically.

"Oh, you're an *awful* pessimist, Kit!" sighed Caroline. "But never mind. Pour as much cold water on everything as you like. This afternoon we'll find out who's right!"

But they didn't. For at half past one it started to snow. Just a few big flakes at first, floating leisurely down like curling goosefeathers; then more and more, smaller ones, fighting furiously together in the gray air and fluttering softly against the windowpanes like stealthy footsteps. The children watched it as they ploughed their way through Mrs. Tidy's suet pudding (helped out with generous lacings of golden syrup), and Richard remarked gloomily that it looked as if it had come to stay.

"With that sky and the wind in the north-northeast nothing could be more certain," agreed Aunt Amethyst, regarding the dirty gray heavens with disfavor. "It's coming in straight from the moor."

"We were going exploring this afternoon," sighed Caroline despondently.

"Well, you won't now, that's clear." Aunt Amethyst looked stern. "But we'll make up a big fire and we'll roast chestnuts and play checkers and chess and such."

Which is just what they did. Kit even had a music lesson and while this was in progress Caroline and Richard went to the library to see if they could summon Michael. He was not forthcoming, however; the snowstorm looked dull and uninteresting, the room was bitterly cold and, to clinch matters, when (as it grew dusk) they went to switch on the light they found that it had fused. All in all, they were glad to get back to the warm and cheerful anteroom. It was still snowing when they went to bed.

Next morning it had stopped, however, and the sun was out, glistening with fiery brilliance on the frosted windowpanes. The dazzling white snow was tinted blue in the shadows, etched with silver and gold in the sunlight—and Aunt Amethyst and Fauntleroy had driven to market, leaving deep curving tracks in the drive.

The children, kneeling on the window seat after breakfast, looked out with wonder at the colorful scene. All manner of red and green and gold tints were brought out in the tree trunks from the reflection of the snow; the feathery branches of silver birches were colored a faint purple. Bracken in far-off woodland glades showed bronze and orange; the distant moors were softly violet. Over all the clear, shell-like sky was a delicate and beautiful blue "Cerulean blue," noted Caroline, dreamily. The cold air was keen and sharp as a knife, but fresh and sweet with an almost spring-like fragrance.

They could see now that there were prints of birds and animals all over the lawn, and they tried to recognize them. There were networks of rabbit tracks and patterns of tiny footprints left by rats, easily distinguishable from those of mice by the long dragging tails. But all these they had seen before. There was one track they could not place, but it was probably that of a fox, Richard observed, for in its wake was a sorry trail of feathers—a pheasant's, perhaps. . . .

So intent were they on reading these hieroglyphics in the snow that they did not notice the lowering gray clouds creeping up on the sun from behind the house, and the first returning snowflakes took them by surprise. Almost in the same moment the golden sunshine vanished and they looked up to see Caroline's cerulean blue being rapidly blotted out by a dirty gray pall.

The change of scene was almost dramatic. Within a few moments everything they had been admiring was veiled in white. Running to the back of the house they found the familiar landscape of fields and woods and moorland beyond the garden already completely invisible. A few minutes more and even the garden was lost.

At the same time there came the reassuring trundling sound that heralded Dooley and his wheelbarrow. He had been busy for an hour or more clearing paths around the house and the barrow was laden with spades and shovels of various sizes.

"Do you think it's going to keep it up, Mr. Dooley?" queried Kit.

"That I do, missie. Be snowed in soon, we will."

"Aunt Amethyst has gone to market," said Caroline anxiously, "and on the way back she has some errand in the village. I do hope she'll get home all right."

For a moment Dooley looked as if that had him worried. Then his face broke into a broad grin. "I never heard of Miss Amethyst not getting back from anywhere! She'll get home all right, my dears, if she has to crawl on her hands and knees, so don't ye go a-worriting. . . . If it weren't that Mrs. Dooley be laid up along o' her rheumaticks I'd bide a while. But Mrs. Tidy'll be here soon to cook for ye, and she'll be a bit a company for 'ee."

He stamped and shook the snow off his boots in great clods and put his spades and shovels on the porch ready for next time. Presently they saw him going off home.

The snow, as Dooley had predicted, did not let up. Thicker and thicker it fell, drifting in under the dairy door and piling on the windowsills, even finding its way down the anteroom chimney and making the fire hiss. It was now high time Aunt Amethyst had returned, but she did not come. Neither did Mrs. Tidy arrive to cook the dinner.

"Who could expect her to—in this?" Kit reflected reasonably. "Possibly Aunt Amethyst has arranged to pick her up on her way back. But I'll tell you what: we can start cooking it ourselves. That'll keep us warm and give us something to do to keep our minds off things."

"Good idea!" applauded Richard with enthusiasm. "And let's make it a great meal. Aunt Am is sure to come in with a raging appetite."

"Well, I don't know that it will be awfully exciting," Kit confessed. "We've got to eat the rest of that suet pudding. But there's a perfectly smashing rabbit pie all ready to go in the oven."

"And I could make some chocolate cakes for tea," added Caroline.

In one way and another they were busy all the morning and by the time they had finished it was half past twelve, Aunt Amethyst and Fauntleroy had not returned, and the blizzard was blowing stronger and stronger, the snowdrifts piling up deeper and deeper.

"Supposing something has happened to her—no one will know. Oh, if only we had a phone," lamented Kit.

"I think I ought to go and tell Dooley, or Mrs. Tidy," said Richard uneasily.

"But what could *they* do about it? No more than we could ourselves. And, besides, the snow is blinding—just look at it! You'd only get lost, and that'd be *more* trouble."

They waited another hour and then, at last, hunger driving them from their watch at the window, the three of them sat down to their meal.

Chunky was now as restless as the children, repeatedly leaving his only half-tasted share of the rabbit pie to trot backwards and forwards looking for Fauntleroy. The wind howled down the chimney and the snow went on piling up outside, hiding all the familiar landmarks and even beginning to change the very contours of the garden.

"It's going to be just like in *Lorna Doone*," said Richard. "You know—with the windows bulging and falling right in with the weight of the snow behind them."

"And the kettle freezing by the fire," nodded Kit, gloomily.

"Well, if that's so, we just *can't* sit here eating," Caroline said, suddenly pushing back her plate and leaping to her feet. "I'm going out to see if I can find her."

In the end, of course, all three of them set forth, well wrapped up with woolen helmets and their coat collars turned up around their ears, and armed with sticks, spades, and shovels. Chunky was left behind—he would have sunk up to his nose at the first step, so fine and light was the snow.

Indeed, even the children found it all but impossible to walk in. However, they trudged along in single file, Richard first and the girls following him, the snow getting in their eyes and almost blinding them, pelting them cruelly, mercilessly, with its icy barbs.

Desperately they tried to keep to some sort of definite route, but their legs just would not go where they wanted them to go. Staggering and floundering they managed, with the occasional aid of spade and shovel, to get as far as the avenue, but here, alas, away from the shelter of the house, the drifts were piled up six or more feet high where the snow came driving in from the moors; they shifted and rolled ceaselessly, these drifts, as the wind combed them over and over, and the children found that they were sinking into them at every step.

Another half hour or so of grim struggling with the elements, of calling, and listening, and calling again, and they all had to admit the truth: they were stumped. It went against the grain to have to give up and turn back, but the fact had to be faced: not only would they not find Aunt Amethyst and Fauntleroy—they would get lost themselves.

Dejectedly, half ashamed, they retraced their footsteps. Somehow or other, they found their way back to the house; somehow or other, they floundered around to the back door. Chunky was watching for them at the kitchen window and burst into an ecstasy of relieved barking as they appeared.

They went upstairs and peeled off their wet garments and rubbed their feet and legs until they tingled. Then they went down and stoked up the stove as high as they could and made up the anteroom fire with logs.

"Coal's getting low," observed Richard, coming back from the big coalhouse next door to the dairy. "We'll have to be jolly careful with it."

"It's on order. I heard Aunt Amethyst say so. But nothing is going to be delivered in weather like this, that's clear."

Kit's words echoed ominously in the uneasy silence that followed. No, *nothing* was going to be delivered. Not only coal. There would be no post, no milk (beyond what they might find in the dairy), no groceries . . . nothing! It was a formidable situation.

"Let's hope it leaves off pretty soon," said Richard grimly.

Well, they could *hope*. But there was no sign of it doing so yet.

The afternoon darkened early and they closed the shutters, drew the curtains, and put the kettle on for tea. On second thought they opened the shutters again in case Aunt Amethyst should find her way home and need a light to guide her. Then they made toast and got out the big jar of beef drippings. They had eggs, too, and cut themselves really big slices of cake to keep their spirits up. Caroline's chocolate cakes were smashing, too.

But nothing really could alter the fact that they were alone . . . and anxious.

"You know," said Caroline suddenly that evening, "I've been thinking—why don't we see if the snowstorm can help us? You never know—we *might* be able to find out something about Aunt Amethyst from it. After all, it's magic. . . ."

"Who said it was? It's only our theory. And how *could* it help? Besides, it'll be jolly cold in the library," pointed out Kit.

"Dark, too," nodded Richard, "because the electricity fused. But I think it's a jolly good idea, Caro. I'll get the flashlight, and we'll bring the snowstorm back here."

Caroline jumped up purposefully. "Splendid. Come on, then, Rick! Kit can stay here and wait if she's cold, poor thing."

There were few things that Kit hated more than being referred to as a poor thing, so she quickly joined her brother and sister. They left the anteroom door wide open to afford them more light in the hall, and Richard led the way, flashing his light into the shadows, with the other two close behind.

The library was indeed very cold. As they opened the door it seemed to spring out at them, that cold, and catch them by the throat. Kit sneezed, Caroline turned up the collar of her cardigan and, shivering, they followed the flashlight's small circle of light toward the fireplace. Then, as Richard swept the steady golden beam along the mantelpiece, simultaneously they all exclaimed out loud. For the snowstorm was no longer there!

"Someone must have moved it," said Richard. "Perhaps it's on the desk. . . ."

But it wasn't.

"Well, it must be *somewhere*. Let's search the room."

Caroline fetched a second flashlight and did so. But the fact remained—and after half an hour they had to admit it—the snowstorm had vanished.

Back in the anteroom again, they looked at each other in miserable silence. Each one of them was remembering Aunt Amethyst's words: "There's only one thing of value in the house, and that's the snowstorm."

True, she had said she would never part with it—but grown-ups were known to be fickle. Could one trust her? Certainly it did rather look as if they couldn't.

"Well, that's the end of that idea," said Richard at last, bitterly. "Magic, or no magic, it's gone."

"Unless . . ." hesitated Caroline. "Unless Michael works it from *his* end. He *could*."

"Why, of course!" Richard's eyes were bright again with renewed hope. "He came to us on his own yesterday. *We* can't summon *him*, but he may sense we're in difficulty."

"He may," agreed Kit, "or he may not. But look here, for heaven's sake let's be practical. I vote we sit up all night, so that if the snow stops and Aunt Amethyst gets through we're here to let her in—with a light burning that she'll have seen from a long way off, and a big fire, and something piping hot to drink."

Certainly it was a good idea. Moreover, it was a distinct relief to be *doing* something again. They brought down blankets, eiderdowns, and pillows from their beds and at nine o'clock, having stoked up the boiler for the night, they wrapped themselves in the blankets and made themselves comfortable around the hearth. "We can take turns sleeping," suggested Richard. "One at a time would be best—don't you think?—with the other two keeping watch and making up the fire."

"Just the thing," agreed Kit and Caroline.

And so the long night passed away, and when dawn came the blizzard had passed, too. But the snow was as high as the windowsills now, and the three children were still alone in the house.

Chapter 13

DISCOVERIES

At breakfast, over eggs and bread-and-milk and steaming coffee, Caroline, Kit, and Richard planned their morning.

They would have to save their meager supply of coal for the boiler, they decided, and only use wood in the anteroom—so, first of all, they must clear a path to the woodhouse and bring in all the logs they could. Then they would light a fire in Aunt Amethyst's bedroom (they knew it was safe to do so, for she had told them herself that she sometimes lit one there in cold weather) and put a hot-water bottle in her bed. After that, as Richard remarked hopefully, it would no doubt be time for the next meal. "And what will there be?" he inquired anxiously. "We've eaten the rabbit pie."

They all went to the pantry and inspected its shelves with some concern. There were two loaves of home-made bread, a bin full of flour, and a side of bacon hung up on one wall. There were sacks of potatoes and the remains of the vegetables they had used yesterday. There were also rows and rows of jams and jellies which their aunt had made the previous summer: plum, apple, straw-berry and raspberry, marrow-and-ginger, rhubarb, and black currant. Wild fruits of the moors and hedgerows as well—blackberry, crab apple, sloe, and bilberry. Last, but not least, there was, of course, the old red crock full of eggs. In the dairy beyond they found pats of butter, a tall pitcher of milk, a bowl of cream, and even a round cheese in the old cheese press, for Aunt Amethyst made her own.

"Well, we won't starve, anyway," observed Caroline in relief, as they returned to the kitchen. "And then there are all those apples in the attic, too."

"So now to work." Kit nodded.

Once more their heavy overcoats went on, and their knitted hoods, their boots and their warmest gloves, and out they went into the snow. There was quite a weight of it against the back door, they found, for it had drifted into the stone porch, deep though that was. The spades they had used yesterday, however, were fairly dry in one corner and they took turns using them, shoveling the snow away in front of them and piling it up high on either side. It was stiff work, they discovered as they progressed, but after an hour or so a narrow pathway— it looked more like a deep ditch with steep banks—had been achieved as far as the woodshed, and their labors

were at an end. Or so they thought. But alas, a calamity
awaited them: the door was locked and they did not
know where to find the key.

"Unless it's one of those hung up on the key board in
the kitchen?" suggested Kit.

"It'd have to be a larger key than any of those, I should
think. Still, we can try." And Richard turned back to
the house. "I'll fetch them all."

He fetched them in vain, though, for he was quite
right—they were all too small.

"If only it had a window we could break it and climb
through," reflected Caroline.

But it had no windows at all.

They did manage to force their way into the adjoining
coachhouse, for the door was not locked, but there also
they drew a blank. There was not a sign of a key anywhere, nor was there an inner door giving access to the
woodhouse, as Kit seemed to think she had noticed there
was.

"Guess we've had it," said Richard glumly.

"But what on earth are we going to do? We *must* have
wood, or there won't be enough coal to last."

It was then that Richard had his bright idea. He happened to glance up at the loft—and suddenly he whistled.
"I've got it! All that old junk up there! Those old chests
and all that other clutter! We'll chop it up and use *that!*"

"Rick!" exclaimed Caroline, shocked. "We can't do a
thing like that!"

"Can't we? You haven't seen it, Caro! You didn't
come up. It's of no earthly use to anyone, my dear
girl, or it wouldn't be up there. It's all rotted away any-

way—I noticed that specially before I spoke up."

"So it is," agreed Kit warmly. "I think it's a grand idea. After all, Caroline, we've got to keep the fires going and if we haven't anything to do it with we've just got to be resourceful and *find* something. Besides, I've just remembered—Aunt Amethyst said herself that it all had to be cleared out some day."

"And that day has come," said Richard blithely, starting off up the stone steps. "Come on, Caro, you'll have to come too this time. No staying down below and putting us off with your seeing things. Look—there are iron staples in the wall here and there. You can hold onto those if you feel dizzy."

Caroline hesitated, but the prospect of climbing the narrow stairway was not nearly as frightening, somehow, as that of being left alone below, and so she set her teeth and followed grimly after Richard, with Kit safely bringing up the rear.

In the loft a rat scuttled away at their approach as it had done on their previous visit. There, just the same, were the mildewy bursting sacks, the blotched mirrors, the queer distorted shapes of ancient furniture looming up out of the shadows.

"See!" said Richard. He moved an old chair and the sawdust fell away even as he touched it, so worm-eaten was it. "What good would that be to anyone?"

"No good at all," agreed Caroline. "Only . . ."

"Only nothing. Come on. We can't waste time quibbling. We've got to get this stuff into the house before the snow starts again."

"How are we going to get it down?"

"Easy," said Richard, firmly sweeping away all difficulties. "We'll just tip it over the edge—that will break it up nicely for us. The rest—the chopping up small—we can do indoors."

Caroline and Kit looked at him admiringly. Certainly he had something there.

"Right!" chuckled Kit. "What first? The chair?"

For answer—"Crash!" went the chair over the edge. They peered down and saw that it had indeed broken into several pieces.

"Good! Now—What next?"

"This old table, and then the chest of drawers behind it."

They dragged the table out, and Richard trundled it along toward the precipice before letting it fall heavily onto the ground below.

They took out all the drawers in the big chest, and they went over, too. It was not so easy to move the old chest itself, so massive was it, but with all three of them pushing and pulling they managed it at last—and it fell with the biggest crash of all.

By this time they had almost forgotten that they were snowed up, and were all quite enjoying themselves. They had almost forgotten Aunt Amethyst, too, for the moment.

"This cheese press next?" queried Kit, dubiously. "It's like the one in the dairy."

"Perhaps we had better leave that," conceded Richard, "You never know—that *might* be some use."

"Don't you think we've got enough now?" Caroline suggested. "Look! It's started to snow, again."

It had—and heavily, too.

"Well, let's just have a last look around and see how much more we can use, and then we'll be off." Richard probed further into the cobwebby depths of the loft and observed with satisfaction to his sisters that there was enough old junk to last for years. "Old beds, old wooden chests, old footstools and cradles . . . you never did see. Hello! What's this! Gosh—come and look! Don't tell me it's the sedan chair!"

But it was! *A* sedan chair, anyway. . . . Perhaps once its hangings *had* been rose-colored; they were gray now, and hanging in rotting shreds. Perhaps once its lanterns *had* been brightly gilded—they were black now, and the leather strips were green with mildew. But it *was* a sedan chair.

"Shades of Lady Laetitia!" whistled Richard.

For a moment they all stood looking at it in awed silence. Then Kit said with a wicked grin, "I wonder if the seat lifts up! Go on, Rick, you can try now—and it won't be violation!"

"By Jupiter! So I can!" Richard's eyes fairly sparkled. "Look! The cushions are all rotten and eaten away— moths, I suppose, and mice. . . . Wow!" Richard sprang back hastily for there *were* the mice: a mother and a father and a whole nestful of babies, scrambling here, there, and everywhere in squeaking fright. Kit and Caroline beat a hasty retreat, too. Not that they were scared, as Kit said afterwards, but—well, *mice!*

"Give them a few moments and they'll all be gone," advised Richard. "They'd better, anyway, for I'm going to try that seat this time, even if I'm overrun with vermin."

"Well, hurry!" said Caroline. "It's snowing like anything now."

"Oh, *bother* the beastly snow! Look here, this may be important. I *won't* be hustled. Hah—that's the last one gone, poor little beggar. . . . Now let's see. By gosh! It does—it *does* lift—and look . . . *look!*"

"What is it? Oh, get out of the way, Rick, and let us *see!* What is it? Is it the coins?"

"No, it's not the coins, but, gosh—would you believe it! It's Lady Laetitia's fan!"

And sure enough, Richard backed out of the sedan chair holding up the elegant ivory instrument that had rapped Kit's knuckles so effectively.

"It *is*, isn't it?" demanded Richard.

"Yes. *I* ought to know," nodded Kit.

"That's wonderful!" breathed Caroline. "And it's not broken or anything? It opens out all right? Yes, so it does. My! Isn't it super!"

For a moment they stood in silence, gently opening and shutting their dainty treasure.

"I suppose this one is the ivory brisé, as Aunt Am called it. I don't," observed Richard with masculine vagueness, "know much about women's clutter myself, but I reckon it's pretty valuable."

"She mentioned another one," recalled Caroline. "One that had been painted by Watteau . . . Wasn't there a rumor that it had once belonged to a queen . . . Marie Antoinette, wasn't it? That would be valuable! Is there another one in there by any chance, Rick?"

"By golly, isn't this enough? No, there's nothing else," Richard reported. "Only cobwebs and spiders. Well, the mice can come back now." And he let down the lid.

"How *thrilled* Aunt Amethyst will be!" said Caroline.

At the thought of Aunt Amethyst they all fell silent, and the fact that it was snowing and that there was much to do reasserted itself.

"Let me have the fan, Caro," suggested Richard. "My pocket is deeper than yours—it will be safer." He tucked it away carefully. "Well, now we've got to cart this wood home."

Caroline had been wondering how she was going to get down those steps again, but the excitement of finding the fan seemed to have chased her anxiety right out of her mind and she was down them before she had even thought about it.

They each loaded themselves with as much wood as they could carry and set out for the house with Chunky bringing up the rear—carrying his share in his mouth.

"It will mean two or three journeys," observed Richard, "and don't let's forget the hatchet, whatever we do."

They dumped their booty in a pile in the scullery and set off again. Actually five journeys proved necessary and by the time everything was safely indoors, the drifting snow was fast filling up their pathway again and the sky was heavy and yellow with more to come.

"Never mind, we've got quite enough to go on with; the job has made us warm—and now it's dinnertime."

Kit opened the kitchen door as she spoke and then drew back with a smothered exclamation.

At the table stood a little girl. She wore a white cap and a long full-skirted gray dress with a large white apron over it. A hornbook hung from her waist. Beside her was a curly-haired little boy wearing a long-skirted coat and, even as the children stood there, rooted to the spot, a door beside the fireplace opened and another older boy came in. He wore a green doublet, hose and breeches, buckled shoes, a sword belt of green leather, and a little sword with a silver hilt. His high-crowned hat matched his suit and had a gray feather in it.

The large-raftered room was not unrecognizable. The long dresser was still there, though in place of the cups and saucers and the big dinner service there were gray pewter plates and dishes, polished drinking horns, posset cups and flagons, wooden bowls, and brass and pewter pans. The sturdy table in the middle of the room, spotlessly scrubbed and sanded, looked familiar, too. But the great black range with its ovens and hobs and big brass fender had vanished—instead a roaring fire leapt and crackled on the hearth and there was an appetizing smell of roasting and baking meats—geese and capons—turned on a spit by an old servingman. The floor was strewn with rushes.

Caroline, Kit, and Richard did not move or speak. Indeed, they felt as if they were invisible, for no one appeared to have seen them.

Then someone spoke.

"Thou call'st me?" said the boy in the green doublet, who had come through the door by the hearth (where no door was today, reflected Caroline).

Before anyone could answer, before the children could

even so much as open their mouths, suddenly Chunky
came bounding in behind them and, seeing the strange
occupants of the kitchen, immediately turned tail and
began to howl.

At once they all vanished like shadows—children,
servingman, and all—the kitchen became familiar again,
even the very light seemed clearer. . . .

"Before we could even so much as exchange a good day
with them," grumbled Richard, who had been thrilled
stiff. "A pox on you, Chunky, for an ill-mannered
hound."

Kit was not so sure that she minded. "I don't think I
like it," she said, with a little shiver. "I wish we had the
house to ourselves—and that Aunt Amethyst would come
back."

"Well, never mind. Don't have a wishbone where your
backbone ought to be. Come on and let's get something
to eat," consoled Caroline. "Let's have bacon and eggs."

"And baked apples," added Richard. "My word, I
could do with some of that roast goose they had! Perhaps
they'll come back. . . ."

But, to the secret relief of the girls, if not of Richard,
nothing else happened, and they spent the afternoon
chopping up their wood.

The anteroom fire had burned low while they had
been outside. They piled it high with their "logs," placed
the brass fireguard in front, and went up to Aunt Amethyst's bedroom to light a fire there. It was not easy, the
chimney was damp, but at last they got it going. Kit put
a hot-water bottle in the bed and they drew the curtains
ready for the night. Quite cozy it looked then, with the

white light of the snow blotted out and the firelight sending shadows over the walls.

"Now that we've got it all ready for her she'll surely come," said Caroline wistfully as they went downstairs again.

Chapter 14

TREASURE TROVE

But she didn't come.

And so they found themselves in the anteroom again, with another anxious night in front of them.

Kit suddenly shivered. "Oh, it's cold! Let's pile as much wood on the fire as we can—even if we set the chimney afire."

They all sat and stared into the heart of the leaping flames in silence for a while. Then Richard got up and paced around the room restlessly. "The time has come for us to do some straight thinking," he said tersely.

"Explain yourself, boy," demanded Kit, giving him a withering look.

"Well," began Richard, coming back to the fireside and sitting down again, quite oblivious of all sarcasm. "It seems to me that everything that has happened to us since we arrived here has been so queer that there must in some way be a purpose in it all."

"Such as?" queried Kit in superior tones.

"Well, it must have been positively *meant* that we should pick up the snowstorm and discover the magic in it. We were supposed to learn something from it. How there's nothing in time and space, perhaps? Michael found it out, and now *we* know it, too. Do you remember that quotation we memorized once and used as an incantation, hoping it might work magic? How did it go? *'Time and space are only forms of thought. . . .'* "

Caroline nodded. "I remember. *'Time and space are only forms of thought. . . . If we were only made the right way we could see everything happening in the same place at the same time.'* That was it."

"Yes. Well, I don't know where we got it from, but anyway it's what I'm trying to say."

"I know where we got it from: one of the E. Nesbit books. I forget which one."

"The Story of the Amulet, if I'm not mistaken," supplied Kit, "but it beats me, Rick, what you think we're going to learn, and how it's going to help us, anyway, if we did. What exactly are you getting at?"

"Well, I guess it all does sound a bit farfetched," admitted Richard, "but I think that all these folks we've been meeting—Michael and all the others, and even those children we saw in the kitchen today—are out to help us, if only we could see it. They want to help us save Farthingales, for one thing. They all loved it, same as Michael did, same as Aunt Amethyst does, same as we do—and they don't want to see it fall into ruin. Quite apart from that, I've got a hunch those kids in the kitchen today could have put us onto Aunt Amethyst in some way, if only Chunky hadn't gone and messed everything up."

Hearing his name, Chunky looked up from the hearth-rug and thumped his tail uncertainly. Kit fondled his ears.

"How on earth could they?"

"I don't know—call me bighead if you like, but I'm sure I'm somehow right."

Caroline was looking thoughtful. "And how could they—any of them—help us save Farthingales, Rick? In what way?"

"Well, Michael told us about the coins, didn't he? And then, whether she knew it or not, Lady Laetitia gave us a hint where to find the fan. I've just remembered that secret drawer in the desk that Michael showed us— we can look for that tomorrow and see if the miniatures are back there again."

"And the secret passage from the gazebo—does that come in anywhere?"

"It could. I don't know. . . . But it's all part of what we have to learn, for some reason or other."

"Well, anyway, say you're right," criticized Kit. "The only thing that has materialized so far, help or no help, is the ivory fan."

"But it will come," persisted Richard. "I'm dead sure of it. Now that the snowstorm has gone we've got to think out what everything means."

"Oh, it's beyond me," said Kit irritably. "I'm sure none

of it means anything at all. I'd rather it didn't, anyway. My head feels as if it's got iron bands around it that I can't burst."

"And I feel as if I'm tied to a great wheel that never stops turning." Caroline looked rueful. "That's what your time theory does for you, Rick. We've got caught up in the past too much. It leaps out at us at every turn. This morning, for instance—what purpose could there have been in that?"

"And maybe tonight or tomorrow there'll be something or somebody else. It's got out of hand—it's too much altogether."

Richard remained silent, looking doubtfully at his sisters.

"I think we're tired of it," Caroline went on. "We want to lead our ordinary lives. Instead of bothering about time, why don't we appreciate the present? After all, what could be more exciting than what has happened to us? We're alone and snowed up in a ramshackle old house that we've got to keep warm and dry. It will never happen to us again, most likely. Why don't we make the most of it? It's thrilling, really."

"Except that Aunt Amethyst is lost," reminded Kit.

"And Fauntleroy," added Richard glumly.

"If only your theory *could* help us find them, Rick, there might be something in it," conceded Kit, relenting.

They all sat in silence for a while, and then Caroline said suddenly, "You know, I believe even old Burbage comes into it somehow. I've been thinking of him a lot— I think he's at the bottom of all those missing things— the coins and everything. Michael said Burbage was a

wicked old man—and he couldn't believe Mr. Allardyce
was a thief. What if it were he—Burbage—who stole
them? Who was feathering his nest? He was coachman
and Mrs. Burbage was housekeeper. . . . Perhaps she was
in it, too? She had her eye on this and that, and she
would quietly pass them on to old Burbage, who'd hide
them away somewhere until he could dispose of them—
and why not in the loft? What could be easier, with that
corridor running along from the green baize door in the
servants' quarters, as Michael described to us. And we
have already found the fan up there."

"But I shouldn't think that the fan was *stolen*, would
you? Surely a sedan chair is a natural enough place for a
fan to be lost in—and found in?"

"Well, yes. But what if we find the coins up there, too
—and the miniatures?"

Richard whistled. "It's a smart idea, anyway."

"Tomorrow," said Caroline urgently, "instead of
breaking everything up, let's *search* it—thoroughly. Because I'm certain I saw old Burbage for some good
purpose, as Rick would say!"

"Right! Then that's tomorrow's program," grinned
Richard. "I bet we'll have to dig out our path all over
again, though."

"Perhaps," agreed Kit, "but it gets us warm."

"Well, if we're going to be so busy tomorrow we'd
best have an early night and be up sharp in the morning.
Let's get the blankets and roll in."

Caroline went to the windows and drew back the
shutters a little way. "I thought I heard something . . .
but I suppose it was only the wind howling. It does

make the most weird noises. It's still snowing—it'll be
up to the eaves tomorrow at this rate."

But it wasn't, for the gale dropped a bit in the night,
the snow ceased, and by breakfast-time next morning the
sun was out and the sky Caroline's cerulean blue again.

Hurrying through their meal and getting into their
overcoats, they made their way out to the garden. "I'll
take the large spade," said Richard, taking it, "and you
girls can have the smaller ones and follow behind."

Thus they embarked upon the task of opening up
their path again and soon the three of them were warm
and rosy with their labors.

"I'd love a game of snowball," said Kit, "but I suppose
we haven't time for sport with such weighty matters on
hand."

"No, we haven't," replied Richard briskly. "Any time
now this sun will go in, you'll see, and it'll start snowing
again."

And just then an enormous snowball caught him on
the ear and knocked off his cap.

"Cheats!" shouted Richard indignantly. "As soon as
my back's turned."

"Cheat my foot," shouted back Kit. "We didn't do it."

"Then who did?"

Kit and Caroline said nothing. They were staring
behind them and suddenly the garden was full of children and the air full of laughter and flying snowballs.

"Here we go again," said Kit in a growly voice. "Someone has been shaking up the snowstorm, I suppose,
wherever it is."

For the children were dressed in strange garments—

doublet and hose, long capes and little bonnets after the manner of children in the days of Elizabeth I. One girl was dressed in blue and she had golden hair. Another younger one wore scarlet, and there was a boy in a gray doublet and hose and another older girl in brown.

"They aren't the children we saw yesterday," observed Richard. "*They* belonged to Cavalier days."

"An earlier vintage, eh?" grinned Kit. "Well, anyway, they don't seem to have spotted us yet."

Certainly these children of long ago did not appear to be aware of the present-day Elizabethans. Richard, it seemed, had had the snowball down his neck quite by accident.

"Like Michael, that first time . . ." recollected Caroline.

"What do you think their purpose is, Rick?" inquired Kit with good-humored sarcasm.

"Couldn't say. But perhaps we'll find out if we watch."

"Watch! Oh, I'm fed up with it all. Let's get on with our path!"

Kit bent to her spade with renewed energy, and at the first scrape and clatter it made on the frozen snow the voices and laughter ceased, and they found they were alone again.

"That's better," said Kit, relieved.

Caroline looked wistful—she had liked the look of the girl in blue—but she said nothing, and presently they had reached the coachhouse and were pushing open its heavy door once more.

"Up we go!" said Richard blithely. "Come on, Caro! We've got a lot to do this morning. Hang onto my belt if you feel funny."

Within a few moments they were all up in the loft.

"And now we search, instead of working destruction," observed Kit, facetiously.

"Yes—but we might just as well tip each thing over the edge as we finish with it," reflected Richard, loth to relinquish yesterday's drama. "Come on, let's try and move this cheese press out of the way a bit—there's all sorts of junk behind it."

And so it started.

Behind the cheese press was an artist's easel, a pair of worm-eaten stepladders, and a seaman's chest. The easel and the ladders were pitched briskly over the edge by a businesslike Richard; Caroline and Kit opened the seaman's chest with the wildest of hopes, but found it empty—so that went over, too. Behind it, in the corner, they found something that was draped with moldering sacking. Pulling the sacking away they discovered a battered mahogany tallboy.

Kit pulled open the top drawer and exclaimed out loud: it was full of tarnished silver!

There were slender candlesticks, a teapot and matching tea caddy, a coffeepot, a little round box standing on three legs and lined with purple velvet, a set of spoons, a silver cup with three handles. . . .

"Cat's whiskers!" exclaimed Richard with a low whistle. "Come on! This is it! Try the others. . . ."

Shaky with excitement, they pulled open the next drawer and there, beneath their fascinated gaze, lay a varied collection of treasures—small gold and enamel trinkets and snuffboxes, gold brooches, rings, a pearl necklace, a small gold bracelet set with rubies.

"*Are* they real gold, do you think?" whispered Caroline.

"Something tells me they are," said Kit, trying to speak calmly. "They wouldn't be here, I guess, if they weren't. Look . . . what's this?"

It was a small bundle wrapped in velvet. Unwinding the velvet they found two miniatures framed in gold. Even the children had not the slightest difficulty in recognizing Mary Queen of Scots—"And the other must be Lord Darnley, then," breathed Caroline.

Speechless, they stared at them.

"You were right, you see, Caroline," said Kit at last.

"Gosh!" agreed Richard, "I'll say she was!" He wrenched open a third drawer. "Oh, only books."

But they were all old books—*very* old, bound in calf and vellum, with queer lettering, and—"There's no 'only' about it," decided Caroline shrewdly. "They're all valuable, every one."

The lower drawers, disappointingly, were empty.

"But what a haul we've got, without anything else," said Richard jubilantly. "My word, it'll just about knock Aunt Am into next week!"

"Let's take it all back to the house right now and clean it up," suggested Kit eagerly. "Then we can have it all set out on show for her when she comes back. It will be a super welcome for her."

"Just the thing," agreed Richard. "I wonder if we could carry the drawers down as they are, or whether they'd be too heavy?"

"Perhaps we could put everything in one of those sacks," mused Caroline, looking at the bags of moldering grain that stood sagging limply against the wall.

"What—those?" scoffed Richard. "Why, they must be rotten right through. They're just as old as they can be." He kicked one of them to prove his point and indeed it was so ancient that it gave way immediately and the mildewy rotten grain poured out in a steady stream across the floor.

Only it *wasn't* grain. Not all of it. . . . "Only on top. Underneath it's gold and silver coins pouring out instead!" cried Caroline, shrill with excitement.

"Jumping Jupiter!" exclaimed Richard. "I *wondered* why the rats hadn't been at it."

All three of them went down on their knees, poring incredulously over their tarnished treasure trove.

The first coin they picked up was a two-guinea piece. It had the date 1678 on it. Another similar one was dated 1693. Then came a Queen Anne five guineas of 1709, a George II five guineas dated 1746 and a number of foreign coins, one of which Richard identified as a Louis Napoleon twenty guilders . . . "A Netherlands coin."

Some of the coins were encased each in a tiny envelope, bearing a faded inscription in a spidery, old-fashioned hand; "Gold royal: Mary Queen of Scots," read one such legend; "James I third coinage: rose royal," declared another, and "Charles I Oxford triple unit: 1642."

There was, of course, absolutely no doubt about it: it was the Faraday Collection.

"Let's put them all in one of the drawers and examine them more closely when we get back," suggested Kit.

"When we've examined the other sacks," said Richard. "Goodness knows what there may be inside them."

But actually the remaining sacks did not yield any further hoard, and all they could find was one Henry VIII gold sovereign that had rolled into a corner.

Somehow, by this time, all three children were feeling strangely tired, and the important thing to do seemed to be to get back to the house as quickly as possible with their wealth of treasure. They piled the coins carefully into one of the empty drawers and gradually, bit by bit, they managed to get everything down the stairs.

There was no snow falling, but the sun had gone in and the wind came sweeping in bitterly from the moor as they crossed the yard. "There'll be more before night-fall, you'll see," said Richard darkly.

But nightfall seemed a long way off. For the moment, indeed, they were far too excited about the morning's events to bother with what might be in store for them later: they had found the Farthingales "treasure" and nothing else had any real importance.

How comfortingly the warmth of the kitchen rushed out at them as they opened the door! It was almost as if it welcomed and congratulated them! They unloaded their precious burden onto the table ("Thank goodness it's our own kitchen this time and we've got it to our-selves!" Kit remarked rather acidly) and set about marshaling their cleaning materials.

"There isn't any silver polish," said Richard, returning from the cupboard.

"I don't suppose there is. Polish costs money," pointed out Caroline. "Anyway, we can manage without—silver-smiths often use wood ash."

Well, they had plenty of that, to be sure. . . .

And so the morning passed away while they cleaned their silver, polished up their gold and laid everything out on the anteroom table ready for Aunt Amethyst's return.

But was Aunt Amethyst ever coming back?

With the last piece of silver set out, the last old book brushed and dusted, the gold and the pearls gleaming in the soft firelight, and the coins stacked in neat, exciting-looking piles, they had to acknowledge they had come to the end.

All the thrill and excitement suddenly went out of their discovery. Without Aunt Amethyst it was, of course, nothing.

She had now been missing for just over two days. True, roads were impassable and drifts twelve feet high in some parts of the West Country, the radio said; but if all was well with her and she was safe and being looked after somewhere, surely *some* means of communication could have been found?

All through their makeshift meal of bread and cheese and omelets and chocolate cakes they debated the urgent question, and at last, with a restless feeling of growing uneasiness that mounted almost to panic, they suddenly knew that they could no longer sit and wait confidently for her safe return. Somehow they knew, as surely as if they had been told, that she was in need of their help. Something had to be done. "And right *now,*" said Richard positively. "We must go in search of her again."

Kit nodded, and gulping down the last of a scalding hot cup of coffee, went to the window. "It's trying to snow again."

"But it's not much," Caroline observed calmly. "And anyway, Richard's right—we *must* go. It has come to that: we've simply *got* to go, even if we get lost and freeze to death."

Chapter 15

THE UNDERGROUND PASSAGE

In a few moments they had on their overcoats and their boots, their woolen hoods and scarves and gloves, and had stepped out determinedly into that silent, crazy, wild-dervish dance of the snowflakes.

They walked straight out of the front door, this time onto hard-packed frozen snow—it was as high as the top step—and Chunky was allowed to accompany them. Richard slammed the door and pocketed the heavy key, and they set off toward the avenue.

Frozen though the snow was, they found that it was still quite difficult to walk once they were out of the shelter of the house, for there the snow was looser. However, they trudged along determinedly, with Chunky following gamely behind, and at last, staggering and floundering, they had reached the long aisle of lime trees.

"Let's start to call straight away," said Kit. "You never know—she could just as easily be close at hand as far away."

Circling their mouths with their hands they all shouted at the top of their voices:

"Aunt *Am*-ethyst! Aunt *Am*-ethyst!"

Then they stopped to listen for an answer—but the spectral wastes only echoed the call back mockingly, the branches of the limes creaked dismally in the bitter wind, and the dizzy, determined dance of the snowflakes seemed even madder and couldn't-care-less than before.

They toiled on, however, stopping to call again from time to time, and while the drive ran between the trees their route was straightforward enough; but presently they reached the point where it left the avenue behind and swept out over the open fields and there, where ditches and ponds and hollows were all of one uniform snowy level with the roadway, it was not so simple to keep their sense of direction.

Kit stumbled and fell into a snowdrift, immediately extricating herself without a word while the others brushed her down.

Then Richard, too, floundered and fell headlong—but unlike Kit he did not at once recover himself. Instead he lay motionless for a moment and when he at last sat up it was to reach forward and feel gingerly in the snow.

"There's something here . . . I don't know what it was I stumbled on, but *something* tripped me up and I fell against something hard. . . . It felt like glass breaking underneath me."

They helped Richard to his feet and all three of them prodded and scraped in the snow with their sticks. Sure enough, presently they encountered something hard, and something else that cracked. They scrabbled and scraped a bit more and at last a third something was uncovered that looked like steel, quite near the surface, where the wind had combed the drift before it froze.

Richard muttered something unintelligible and started digging down furiously. . . . Presently he found that he had uncovered a patch of gray-colored metal.

"It's a car! It's the station wagon!" he exclaimed brokenly.

Too horrified to say a word, Caroline and Kit joined him frantically in his labors and—it was true—gradually Aunt Amethyst's car became visible.

It had evidently skidded into the ditch. It lay there on its side, one window smashed where Richard's weight had fallen on it, but . . .

"But it's empty!" sobbed Caroline in blessed relief. "Oh, thank goodness, it's empty! They did manage to climb out. Look—the door is not quite shut and the snow seeped in—they must have got out and then tried . . . then tried. . . ." Caroline's voice broke and trailed off miserably.

"And tried to reach the house on foot," finished up Kit for her. "Yes. But they didn't. They never got there. So where *are* they—and when did it happen?"

They all looked at each other in despair.

"Somewhere between here and the house, anyway," said Richard quietly. "And it must have been fairly early on."

He circled his mouth with his hands again and the girls quickly followed suit.

"Aunt *Am*-ethyst! Aunt *Am*-ethyst!"

But only the everlasting silence echoed back their call.

"Well, anyway, we do at least know that it's no use going on any further," said Kit. "What we have to do now is to turn back and examine every inch of the way."

"If we *can* turn back," whispered Caroline, white-faced.

"What do you mean?"

Caroline indicated the white swirl around them. "Don't you see how much thicker it is? We can't see more than a yard or two ahead now."

It was true. There was no sign left at all of the distant lime avenue. Every landmark was blotted out as if it had never been. They were lost in a world of spinning snowflakes.

"Well," said Richard, undaunted. "Here's the car. We found it on our left, and we've only to leave it behind on our right to know that we've turned in the proper direction. It's the keeping it up, of course. But at least we can follow our own footsteps."

But even that was not as easy as it sounded, they discovered, so swiftly was the snow obliterating all tracks; and although they stumbled on valiantly, prodding with their sticks as they went, it was really all they could do to keep together, much less search for anyone else.

Caroline, to her dismay, began to flounder every few steps, so sleepy was she becoming, mesmerized by the dizzy spinning and twirling of the white flakes.

Then Richard said anxiously, "I believe we're walking

in circles—you know, like you do in a fog. I'm sure we passed that bush just now."

Kit nodded. "I think so, too. I believe we're lost."

Caroline stumbled and nearly fell again. "How cold it is . . . much worse than it was. And I'm so horribly tired. Couldn't we stop and rest—just for one moment?"

"Not even for one moment," replied Richard firmly. "Whatever we do, we *must* keep moving. I feel just the same, but we've got to fight it."

Richard was right, and they all knew it. Instinctively each one of them realized the danger of yielding to that comfortable drowsiness which was threatening to steal over them.

They plodded on, and stopped to call. Plodded on again, called again.

But still the snowstorm only mocked them and the bitter wind seemed to taunt them, blowing the snow in their eyes, numbing their fingers so that they dropped their sticks again and again. Now their consciousness of time, as well as of distance, was becoming confused. It already seemed as if they had been wandering for hours through the blizzard.

Suddenly Caroline stumbled once more and fell to her knees. Oh, how soft the snow was, she thought bemusedly —soft as a downy pillow, and hardly cold at all, really. . . .

Completely overcome, she sank down into it and immediately her eyes began to close, swiftly, in blessed, heavenly, longed-for sleep. . . .

Vaguely she was aware that Kit and Richard were shaking her violently, even slapping her—but the heavy drowsiness drugged all sensation.

"I don't know what we should have done," reflected Richard later on, "but just then Chunky started barking."

Poor Chunky! He had been keeping up with them so bravely, plunging and leaping along behind them, and now, all at once, he stood stock still with his head raised and gave vent to one of his piercing howls.

It was so penetrating that Caroline rallied at once from her stupor. . . . "I opened my eyes—and there in front of me I saw one of those children we'd seen playing snowballs: the girl in blue. I was so amazed I was awake at once. The others saw her, too."

Yes, the others saw her. "For a moment I thought she was a sort of mirage," Kit recollected afterwards. "But she was waving us forward, and we followed her. We were too tired to wonder if we were doing the right thing or going the right way. She *could* have been a sort of Lorelei beckoning us to our doom, but somehow we knew she wasn't."

They knew she wasn't. They knew that she was there to help them. And then suddenly the other children were with her, too: the boy in the gray doublet and hose, the little one in scarlet, the taller girl in brown . . . all of them laughing and talking and pelting each other with snowballs, though not a sound came from them. The snow went on swirling and the laughing children appeared and disappeared in it like will-o'-the-wisps. . . .

"But they were there, and we followed them," said Caroline reminiscently, "with poor old Chunky tagging along behind, whimpering and dragging his tail."

"None of us had the foggiest idea where we were," added Richard. "I think we'd got past wondering—or worrying. We just took them on trust, as Kit said, and followed after."

Yes, they followed after. And then, suddenly—very suddenly, the blizzard was so thick about them—they saw trees looming up ahead of them and before they knew what they were doing, or where they were, they had walked straight into a bank of rhododendrons.

"Why, it's the Long Grove!" exclaimed Richard.

"The Long Grove?" Caroline could have wept. It was the walls of the house she had longed to see.

But it was true enough. Somehow or other they had by-passed the avenue. The children-of-long-ago seemed to have vanished now, too, and afternoon light was growing dim, the snowfall around them was almost suffocating in its density.

"They *can't* have led us astray. There *must* be some reason for it," said Richard positively. "Come on—let's call again. The loudest yet."

Pulling herself together with a tremendous effort Caroline raised her hands to her mouth and joined in the shout.

"Aunt *Am*-ethyst! Aunt *Am*-ethyst!"

And, for the first time, it seemed as if an answer came out of the white enshrouding gloom.

But it was not Aunt Amethyst.

What they heard was a long, muffled howl, seeming to rise up from the ground at their feet, followed by a frenzied, frantic barking.

"*Fauntleroy!*" they called in thrilled excitement. "*Fauntleroy!*"

Another long-drawn howl followed, and Chunky

started barking and whining urgently in reply, dashing in amongst the bushes and dislodging whole avalanches as he disappeared.

The children plunged in after him, likewise getting the snow down their necks and in their eyes—but there was no sign of a dog anywhere.

Again the muffled howling burst forth, and it still seemed to come from below ground somewhere. Chunky was nosing around and scratching desperately in the snowy undergrowth—could Fauntleroy be caught in a rabbit hole or a fox's earth, or something like that?

"Good show! Dig him out, old man!" applauded Richard. "Where is he, boy? Come on, tell us? Where's Fauntleroy?"

Chunky penetrated a little deeper into the bushes and discovered what appeared to be a small clearing. Here the snow did not appear to have accumulated so deeply and Chunky, scratching and scraping at it, uttering little low, shivering whines of suspense, had soon bared a patch of earth.

Richard pushed his way forward to join him, and for the second time that afternoon tripped over something.

"Now what was *that?*" He held back the branches so that the girls might get through. "I caught my foot in *some*thing, and it felt like . . ."

"A tree root," scoffed Kit irritably.

"No . . ." He scrabbled in the snow and his fingers closed over . . . well, what was it . . . ?

"Gosh!" Richard whistled in shrill triumph. "It's an iron ring! If this isn't a trap door, I'll eat my hat."

"Why, of course—yes, the gazebo!" exclaimed Kit and

Caroline together in simultaneous enlightenment.

And Richard didn't have to eat his hat, because he was right. It *was* a trap door, and, moreover, it opened easily, coming up, a great square slab of stone, as smoothly as if it were oiled; while in the yawning pit that it revealed a flight of steps could be seen leading down, down, down into darkness.

Even before it was fully opened a bounding figure had come leaping up out of that same darkness and Fauntleroy hurled himself upon them in a barking frenzy of affection and relief.

"Good old lad!" cried Richard, throwing his arms around him. "Where's your mistress? Where's Aunt Amethyst?"

Fauntleroy turned and rushed down into the bowels of the earth somewhere and they heard him barking urgently far below.

"She's down there all right." Kit nodded.

"Yes."

Richard got out his flashlight and stepped down resolutely onto the first stair, while Caroline and Kit held their breath in an agony of suspense. But it was all quite safe—the step didn't give way underneath him, he didn't slip on it or tumble headlong into darkness or anything like that—he just went on stepping steadily downward as if it was the most ordinary thing in the world. And presently he evidently reached the bottom, for he shouted up at them that he was down and that it was perfectly O.K. "I'm in a sort of little cellar. It's bricked all around and there's a passage leading out of it. Fauntleroy and Chunky have already gone off along it. The air is all right and there aren't any smells. Coming down?"

"Yes. Coming," said Caroline. "But we're leaving the trap door open. We're not being buried alive. It won't shut up on us—it's too heavy."

Gingerly they stepped down toward the beam of light that Richard flashed up to them. It took them quite a while, but at last they were standing beside him in the little brick-lined cell, their eyes gradually becoming accustomed to the darkness and their feet to the hard, secure feel of brick and stone after the slippery, sliding snow. A chill damp feeling was in the air, quite different from the healthy, if too intense, cold above ground, and a musty, vinegary smell—the sort of smell one came across in old churches, as Kit remarked.

Suddenly something scuttled across the floor. They felt it and heard it rather than saw it, and both girls screamed loudly.

"Heavens!" scoffed Richard. "You'll have the roof in on us if you're not careful. It's only a rat."

"Only!" echoed Kit.

"Well, it's far more scared of us than you have any need to be of it. So come along both of you and don't make such a row."

"You're sure Aunt Amethyst isn't lying collapsed on the floor somewhere?" hesitated Caroline.

Richard's scornful sniff could be heard plainly through the darkness. "Do you think Fauntleroy would have gone dashing off along the passage like that if she had been?" He flashed the light determinedly into the unknown depths ahead. "Come on. The sooner we get out of this the better."

Caroline glanced anxiously at the brick-lined passage as they set off. "Supposing the whole thing falls in on us," she thought. "It must be years since it was last used. . . ."

But the brickwork—at least, what she could see of it— looked as if it had been quite recently newly pointed; the floor seemed to be paved quite smoothly and surely only a rotten coward would think of her own head when poor Aunt Amethyst was probably lying senseless somewhere close at hand?

Richard flashed his light carefully onto the floor and they all walked slowly after the little circle of light, in single file, holding onto each other, and stooping a little because the roof was low. Fauntleroy and Chunky were not very far ahead. Fauntleroy, indeed, was still barking urgently, running back again and again to make sure the children were following. Every now and then a little draft of ice-cold air blew across their heads: there was evidently ample ventilation, although they could not see it.

"I'm just *praying* it leads to the house," said Caroline, "I just *couldn't* face any more snow."

"Well, it *does* lead to the house if it's the passage Michael told us of," pointed out Richard. "And I don't see what else it can be. It seems almost as if it's still in use, too, only there aren't any smugglers nowadays. . . ."

"And, besides, if it leads to the house Aunt Amethyst would have got back to us. Either it doesn't or . . ."

"Or Aunt Am isn't here," concluded Richard. "Well, we'll soon see. I believe we're near the end—I believe we're getting there. Can you smell wood smoke?"

"Yes. . . ."

"Look out—careful! There are some more steps here."
Richard stumbled a bit and fell forward even as he spoke.
There was a sudden tinkle of breaking glass, and the
light went out, leaving them in stifling darkness.

"Oh, golly, now we've had it," Richard's voice sounded
strangely muffled. He felt around for the broken flashlight, but only succeeded in grasping Kit's foot. Not
unnaturally, Kit screamed involuntarily. Caroline caught
her breath and choked back her own cry of alarm, and
for a seemingly endless second or two they all three stood
there in petrified silence.

Then Richard said in rather a small voice, "Well, it's
a bit of luck it didn't happen before. After all, we're
nearly there—I'm sure of it. These steps lead upward.
. . . Come on, grab hold of me, and we'll all go very
carefully."

Up, up, up, they went, slowly, falteringly, with
Richard first exploring every inch of the way with grop-
ing hands and feet; Caroline in the middle, setting her
teeth and telling herself to look *through* the dark and
not *at* it; and Kit manfully bringing up the rear.

They counted twelve steps and then it became obvious
that they were in another passage, higher this time and,
judging by the feel of it, with a vaulted roof. Presently
there was the sound of the dogs' scampering feet somewhere, and Fauntleroy's excited barking and then . . .
what was that? A gleam of light ahead of them? *Could* it
be?

It could. It was. With indescribable relief Caroline,
Kit, and Richard realized that they had indeed reached
the end.

A heavy wooden door confronted them, standing slightly ajar, and in the faint light that shone out they saw Chunky and Fauntleroy come dashing through it, bounding excitedly to meet them.

Hardly daring to breathe, hardly daring to wonder what they would see beyond it, the children pushed the door open. It swung back easily, without creaks or groans, and they found themselves in a small square chamber, stone-walled, stone-floored, and lit by candle-light.

There was a wood fire burning on a rough hearth and in front of it was drawn up a table and a low basket chair. In the chair sat Aunt Amethyst, wrapped in dark gray blankets.

Chapter 16

"PROOF POSITIVE"

"She's asleep," whispered Kit.

Fauntleroy trotted over to his mistress and licked her hand. Then, not receiving any response, he reached up a bit further and licked her face. But Aunt Amethyst did not awaken.

They bent over her anxiously and Caroline gently shook her, but still Aunt Amethyst slept soundly.

"I don't think she's asleep," said Caroline. "She's unconscious. Don't you see . . . it's lack of air and food."

"Yes."

Richard looked searchingly around the room and his eye rested on another door on the far side of the hearth. "I'm going to see what's through there. We've got to get her out of this."

The door opened onto a flight of steps. Richard took a candle and disappeared, and they heard his footsteps going up, up, up. . . . Then silence. But there was the sound of another door being shaken.

"Nothing but doors and steps," muttered Kit. "I'm fed up with it."

Presently Richard reappeared. "The stairs run up to another door, but it's locked." He looked around hopefully. "Anyone see a key anywhere?"

They hunted all around the room, but it didn't yield a key. There were candles, and a small cupboard holding crockery and some old knives and forks. There was a camp bed and a pile of dark gray blankets and a shelf of books. There was Aunt Amethyst's coat, hanging damply on a peg, and her snowboots, placed carefully on their sides to dry. But nowhere was there a key.

"In her pocket?" suggested Kit, going toward the coat.

But all pockets were empty.

On the table a spoon stood in a half-empty box of Ovaltine. Other small items which Aunt Amethyst had apparently brought back from the village with her were grouped together there, too: Sunlight Soap, matches, a jar of Bovril.

"Everything but, in fact," observed Kit.

"Well, when you come to think about it, it stands to reason she can't have had a key," pointed out Caroline. "That's why she couldn't get any further."

It was then that Richard suddenly remembered that he had the front-door key in his own pocket. "It *might* do the trick. It's about the right size."

This time they all went up together. Richard inserted

the key and to their joy it fitted! More than that—it
turned!

It turned—and the door opened into a short passage,
at the end of which was . . . "Oh golly! Not *another*
door!"

Caroline went on ahead. "It's all right. This one's on
a latch."

She lifted it carefully and the door swung heavily back
toward them. In complete silence they stepped through
the small aperture into the comforting warmth of a room
lit only, in the gathering twilight, by a red glow from a
cheery stove. But they needed no stronger light to show
them where they were: it was the kitchen at Farthingales!

"Oh, heaven! *Heaven!*" cried Caroline, with a laugh
that was almost a sob. "Look, let's get the room ready
before we bring her back. I'll put some more coal on
and you fill the kettle, Kit. Then we'll have to see if we
can find some brandy."

Caroline lifted the scuttle and piled on as much of
their precious coal as she dared. Richard had vanished,
but just as the girls were drawing the curtains he reappeared with a box in his hands.

"The first-aid box! I suddenly remembered it! There's
smelling salts and such in it. . . . We'd better take water,
too. And brandy. There's some in the corner closet.
Come on, let's hurry."

Carefully, first, they blocked back the little new-found
door beside the hearth so that it would not close. Then
they ran along the secret passage and down the stairs,
thrilled, excited, their tiredness forgotten, overcome with

the happiness of their wonderful escape.

Aunt Amethyst was still in the same position. They held the smelling salts to her nose—but nothing happened. They splashed water over her face as energetically as she had splashed it over Richard that first day—but still there was no response.

Then Fauntleroy barked and Chunky enthusiastically joined in. "It was enough to awaken the dead!" as Kit said afterwards.

Certainly it awakened Aunt Amethyst—just as, earlier Chunky's howls had roused Caroline. She gave a little sudden, fluttering sigh, and opened her eyes. "Oh . . ." she said weakly, fixing a dazed stare incredulously upon them. "It's you, is it? Thank goodness for that. I'd been wondering," she added wearily, "when you were going to have the sense to come . . ."

Poor Aunt Amethyst!

Somehow they got her to her feet. Somehow or other they helped her up the stairs, Caroline and Kit making a carrying-chair for her with their hands and Richard providing additional support in the rear.

In the warm kitchen the kettle was starting to boil and the lamplight and the firelight joined forces to give the homeliest welcome that ever a band of snow-wanderers had.

Never had a kitchen looked so much like paradise! Never had a bubbling kettle sounded so sweetly on the ears! Never, later on, had scalding hot tea and hot buttered toast tasted so completely ambrosial!

In between mouthfuls of toast and fruit cake, their wet garments removed and themselves cozy and relaxed in bathrobes and slippers, Caroline, Kit, and Richard told their tale.

"But what we'd have done if we hadn't found the secret passage I *don't* know," ended up Richard.

"Secret passage?" Aunt Amethyst looked amused. "There's no secret about that nowadays, lad! Oh, *once . . .* yes, of course. No doubt it's had its moments. The Civil War, for example, and the smugglers. . . . But after that it was unused for years and years—until my brothers and I found it when we were about your age. There was a gazebo in the Long Grove then." She paused, looking back into the past, and the children glanced quickly at each other. "We were playing there one day and we found that a section of the balustrading worked a slab on a pivot in the floor. . . .

"Well, there was money in those far-off days. Your great-grandfather had a whim to put the passage into repair. The floor was paved, the brickwork repainted, the ventilation added. And when World War II came along, the room downstairs there was used as an air-raid shelter. . . . Not that it was ever really necessary, fortunately. But we were prepared. The gazebo had been pulled down by that time, and we'd put in the trap door. Only the estate workers knew about it. Originally it was for their benefit if they—or anyone else working or walking in the gardens were caught in a storm. That was my father's bright idea. Later, one could have said 'if they were caught in an air raid'—but nobody ever was, although I had a narrow escape from a spattering of machine-gun fire on the moors once. . . . But you see how it is. There's no secret about the underground passage. I use it occasionally and I know every inch of it. So, I may say, does Fauntleroy. He loves a good old rat chase down there, don't you, dear boy?"

Aunt Amethyst bent to fondle the dear boy's ears, and he reached up and gave her face a resounding lick from a curly tongue.

"I see," said Richard flatly. And the children all looked at each other rather sadly. How matter-of-fact it all was!

"And you?" said Caroline hesitatingly at last. "We found the station wagon. . . . It overturned, didn't it? You tried to get back on foot, and you thought the underground passage would be quicker—was that it?"

"More or less," confessed Aunt Amethyst, "though I've no wish to recall it, so let's skip it. Actually, I got lost. When I found I was in the Long Grove I realized it was the trap door or nothing. . . . But I was dazed and half silly with shock, I suppose, and it wasn't until I'd reached the room where you found me that I recollected that, of course, the door was locked and I hadn't got the key. Fauntleroy howled, and I shouted and banged on that wretched door till my fists ached . . . but . . . well, you know the rest. . . ."

Yes, they knew the rest. Caroline remembered how she'd thought she heard a strange howling one night and had decided it was the wind. And Richard was recalling how they had seen a boy come through a door beside the hearth in that phantom kitchen—and yet they had never thought to look to see if there *was* one. It had been a straight clue—and yet, for all his talk about everything having a purpose, he'd been completely blind to it!

Aunt Amethyst was staring musingly into the fire.

"But you couldn't know—how could you? I'd never thought to tell you about the passage. It wasn't your fault. Oh, I wondered and wondered how you were faring, you poor mites, and I worried myself nearly sick about you, but it wasn't any use, was it? I tried to go back, but I was too weak after so much wandering to lift up the trap door again from the inside. So I decided to stay where I was till I felt better. The trouble was, I never did. . . . Well, there was plenty of old firewood down there, and so I managed to light a fire. I lived on spoonfuls of Ovaltine and Bovril—neat. Never let me see either again. And Fauntleroy ate up a whole week's supply of dog biscuits: I just hadn't the heart to refuse him. . . .

"Oh, I should have got out eventually, no doubt. But I lost all sense of time down there, and I couldn't keep awake. How long was it, actually?"

"It was three days," said Kit solemnly.

"*Three days!* Good grief! My poor Fauntleroy!" cried Aunt Amethyst, overcome.

It was a topic that was obviously going to last them for weeks. There were questions to ask and to be answered that would take them days and days. But they could all wait.

"Aunt Amethyst, do you think you could manage to get along as far as the anteroom?" asked Caroline presently, after some consultation with the others.

"The anteroom? What for? Isn't it cozy enough here, just for once?"

"Yes . . . but we've something to show you," said Richard. "We've made up the fire, and it's quite warm in there. Kit's gone on ahead to turn the light on. *Do* come, Aunt Am."

Aunt Amethyst looked from one sparkling pair of eyes to another.

"Now what have you three been up to, as soon as my back was turned?"

For answer they gently drew her to her feet; Caroline took her by the arm, Richard led the way, and they conducted Aunt Amethyst toward one of the happiest moments of her life.

There was something special about the anteroom that evening. All the children noticed it. "It seemed to glow," said Caroline afterwards. "It was almost as if it smiled— if a room *can* smile."

"That one did," nodded Kit.

Perhaps the smile was just the gleam of the gold and the silver and the colored enamels laid out on the table; the sparkle of gems, the soft colors of the exquisite miniatures, the shimmer of pearls. . . . Whatever it was, there in the little somber, oak-paneled parlor, the retrieved treasures seemed to glow and throb as if they had a life of their own. The children stood looking down at them with pride and delight, and Aunt Amethyst looked down, too—but uncomprehendingly.

"The lost treasures of Farthingales," said Caroline softly.

"The *what?* I've *told* you. There's no such thing, child."

Aunt Amethyst's voice was sharp. Then it trailed off into silent stupefaction. For after all, there was no longer any denying it.

"There it *was,* before my very eyes," as she told a spell-bound Dooley and an equally speechless Mrs. Tidy a few days later. "At first I thought the brandy must have gone to my head. Then, bit by bit, I recognized it all—recognized it from this rumor and that, from family tales handed down from generation to generation, tales heard and remembered, but never really believed. . . ."

No, never really believed. . . . Not until now, this wonderful evening in the anteroom, with the proof all laid out solidly before her—"Positive proof," as Richard said, grinning broadly.

"Positive proof, indeed," agreed Aunt Amethyst dryly. "And now tell me how you came by it, you young marvels, you!"

She listened in amazed silence while the children, first one and then another of them, told their tale. She applauded Richard's presence of mind in deciding to break up her old furniture for firewood, and she thrilled with them over the discovery of the treasure-filled drawers and the Faraday Collection. She would even have understood about Michael, they felt, had they told her about him. But once again something kept them silent and by instinctive common consent they did not mention him. When at last they had finished the story Aunt Amethyst did not speak for quite a while. Then, like one emerging from a trance, "Yes, it all comes back to me now," she admitted dreamily.

"The stories I used to hear as a child, and talk over with my brothers, and the rumors about the Burbages in my great-great-grandfather's day, which had persisted over the years. They were trusted servants, and respected, those Burbages. But Robert Allardyce, the tutor, always contended that they were feathering their nests. It seems he used to roam about the house at dead of night, hoping to catch them red-handed. Of course, he never did—no doubt they were far too clever, and no one ever really believed him, poor boy. Not even Amethyst."

"Amethyst?"

"The old man's daughter. My great-great-aunt. I was named after her. Robert Allardyce was devoted to her— he wanted to marry her." Aunt Amethyst looked sad for a moment. "Poor boy," she repeated softly. "Again—he never did."

"Why was there a tutor here?" asked Kit with well-simulated curiosity.

Aunt Amethyst looked at her speculatively. "He was here for young Michael, who lived at Farthingales while his parents were in India. They never came back, and Michael . . ."

"Yes . . . what happened to Michael?" asked Richard almost inaudibly.

"Michael died when he was twelve years old. There was a rumor . . ."

"Yes . . . there was a rumor?" prompted Caroline gently.

"That Michael is still here . . . sometimes."

There was complete silence in the room for a moment.

"And that reminds me," added Aunt Amethyst at last, unbuttoning the leather jacket she wore and feeling in an inner pocket. "I called to see the vicar on my way back. That's how it was I got caught in the blizzard actually, and I suppose you could say it served me right, but I was becoming desperate, and I wanted him to take something up to Sotheby's for me. . . . Well, fortunately, as it turns out, the dear man was already *in* London—and now, of course, I shan't *have* to part with it."

As she spoke she was unwrapping a small parcel.

"Just run along to the library with it, Richard, will you? It goes on the mantelpiece, on one side of the clock, and somehow I don't *think*," added Aunt Amethyst judiciously, "that it ever ought to be moved again."

Beaming, she held out a small, sparkling object—and every eye was upon the mysterious treasure as it changed hands.

Then Caroline, Kit, and Richard exchanged secret smiles.

It was, of course, the snowstorm.

MONEY CONVERSION TABLE

pound (£)	$2.40
guinea	$2.54
crown	$0.60
shilling	$0.12
pence	$0.01

ABOUT THE AUTHOR

Beryl Netherclift was brought up on a farm in Wivelsfield, England. A member of the Society of Authors for the last twenty-five years, she has previously published two books and numerous articles. THE SNOWSTORM stems from her interest in old houses, which she enthusiastically visits all over the English countryside, and a snowstorm paperweight containing a replica of Westminster Abbey that was given to her as a gift. This is her first book on the Knopf list.

Text set in Baskerville
Composed and bound by The Book Press Incorporated,
Brattleboro, Vermont
Printed by Halliday Lithograph Corporation,
West Hanover, Massachusetts
Typography by Jane Byers Bierhorst